I0554034

Witch Risen

A Paranormal Adventure
Bad Tom Series: Book Two

Jill Nojack

IndieHeart Press
Kent, Ohio

Cover and interior designed by IndieHeart Press.

www.jillnojack.com

Witch Risen / Jill Nojack. -- 1st ed.
ISBN: 978-0-9911234-7-6

THE SHIFT IS BRIEF. It always is. My long human body shrinks, warps, and folds into itself until the cat is revealed.

I launch away as soon as Cat's feet hit the floor. I can't tell what that vile witch Eunice is doing behind me in the attic, but I bet her smirk still lingers on Cassie's hijacked lips. I bet she believes I'll welcome her back with a purr and a brush against her legs.

This is my only shot to escape: when she gets up to speed, she'll throw some magic at the attic door to slam it, and I'll never escape her again. All I can do is hope she hasn't gotten a groove going with her stolen body yet.

But she doesn't spell it shut: I'm down the stairs, I'm across the hall, I'm into the parlor, I'm across the sill, I'm shimmying down the tree trunk,

I'm over the fence, and I'm tearing through the backyards of Giles toward Gilly's house with fear as my running companion.

I need witches.

Powerful witches.

And I need them now.

When I get there, the house is dark and the car isn't in the drive. Where do I go from here?

Natalie. Yes. She was there when I needed help to gain the ability to control my shifting. But that's miles away.

It doesn't matter: I have to keep going. It's Cassie who is really at stake. I can't fail her.

I urge Cat on, and his shadow races ahead as we pass under the glow of a street lamp. Cat is fast, but he's going to be out of gas soon. I think about shifting to move faster on my long, human legs, but I reject the idea of running through town naked and barefoot almost as soon as it comes to me. Even the cops in a witch-ruled town like Giles might have a problem with that one. The thought of losing Cassie because I'm in jail for indecent exposure keeps me gliding forward on Cat's silent feet.

Nat's house is brightly lit. I jump to the sill at an open window and wail in the tone Cat saves to make humans pay attention, the one that sounds eerily like a baby's cry, but it's drowned out by music and laughter. Wait...that's Gillian's laugh. I'd know that happy sound anywhere, even though it's slipped a few notes down the musical scale over the years. I glance toward the street—Gilly's car is parked there with Robert's behind it.

Whatever they're doing, whoever is with them, I'm crashing the party. It doesn't matter who sees me shift from cat to man today: Cassie is in mortal danger. I use the last of Cat's flagging energy to tear through the screen with sharp claws and push my head, then my upper body, through. I shove as hard as I can, rending the hole wider for the rest of Cat's body as I go. I hit the floor and keep moving toward the sound of "Go Ask Alice" blasting from the stereo.

They're sitting around a wooden card table in the front parlor. Natalie's wearing a green dealer's visor over her platinum hair, and her ever-present red vinyl handbag sits on the floor beside her. She's overdressed for a poker party at home in a flattering black pantsuit. She chomps on a huge cigar while she leans in to the card table and deals the cards. Gillian and Robert watch her hands closely. They'd have to. You can never really trust Nat with the small things. She's reliable with the big ones, though.

I think my words, *good Tom*, and furry black limbs turn smooth and beige as they stretch and grow, forming from cat to man in the space of only heartbeats. Shifting always causes pain as limbs expand and joints crack and break until they reshape themselves into something new. I can't help but whimper, although I try to hold it in, and it ends up escaping in a high-pitched yelp before I'm fully formed.

Gilly's head snaps toward me at the sound. I can see that I startled her as my vision adjusts from a cat's slits to a man's round irises. "Tom? What are you doing here?"

Two more heads turn toward me. Robert exudes calm, his usual state. Nat is always hard to read.

When my muscles release from the sharp pain of being stretched beyond capacity to lingering stiffness, and my body fully settles into its human shape, I snug my legs against my torso and wrap my arms around my knees to preserve as much dignity as I can. Like that's going to help when I've just landed in the middle of a senior citizen's living room in my birthday suit.

"It's Cassie. Eunice has her." Once I say it, once I'm firing on all my human cylinders, it sounds so desperately real. Natalie's house is that steamy, old-lady warm, but I feel very, very cold.

Nat gets up and heads toward the hallway, muttering as she goes. "Couldn't just be a fun little strip show. There always has to be drama." She sighs as she disappears around the corner.

Gilly says, "Tom, we buried her. The whole bloody town showed up just to make sure she was really dead. What do you mean she has Cassie?"

"She's taken her body. Eunice is *wearing* her."

Nat reappears next to me with a frilly pink robe. She's baiting me, I'm sure, but I put it on without hesitation to cover myself and take the fourth chair at the table. I don't have time for her games. I'd cover myself with a lampshade if that's what she handed me.

I don't miss a beat as I continue. "Cassie picked up an old clay box and read the words on it...and then Eunice just...took her." As I talk, I pick up a stack of cards and snap the ones on the top of the deck against the ones on the bottom until Gillian puts her hand across mine and gently takes them away. "She shifted me after making sure I knew it was her, and I ran. All I could think was that I needed help to undo whatever she'd done to Cassie, so I left Cassie to her, and I ran." It really, truly hits me then. I drop my head into my hands, overcome by what I'd done. "Goddess, help her. I abandoned her."

"It can't be her. No, it can't be," Robert insists. I look up to meet his eyes, and he's unruffled and impeccably dressed despite a string of empties marching along the edge of the table by his right hand.

"It. Was. Eunice." There's more anger in my voice than I mean to put there. "Now, please tell me that one of you potent witches knows how to get Cassie back."

***

Natalie takes charge. It always surprises me

when she moves into the leadership role. I should expect it; she's been the coven's high priestess since Eunice died, but her steadiness when at the helm is completely at odds with her eccentric old lady act.

She hands me a hot cup of fragrant mint tea in a stoneware mug. "Tell it to us from the beginning, Tom. Don't leave anything out. We need to hear every detail." Her slightly blood-shot brown eyes project command.

In this case, I'll let her lead me. I'm too scattered to begin developing a plan. Telling it as it happened may trigger something that lets me start to figure it out.

Two witches and a warlock hang on my every word as I begin.

"We'd just decided tonight to reopen Cat's Magical Shoppe tomorrow after we...well, we've been together for the past few days as more than roommates." Heads nod. Gilly smiles.

"I hadn't taken Cat out to hunt for a while, and he needed it so that I don't start pouncing at birds in public. I went out to Corey Woods to hunt, and when I came back, I couldn't find her. I heard a noise in the attic and found her up there, shuffling Eunice's things around. She said it was about time she got around to it. Everything seemed fine."

I stop to think, and Nat says, "Good. Stay focused as it gets more difficult. How did it go wrong?"

I squeeze my eyes shut, trying not to lose myself

to the image of the blue-gray smoke that wasn't smoke. "She'd just put down a brooch after I stopped her from putting it on. I said one of you guys should check it out to make sure Eunice hadn't left any booby traps. And Cass agreed with me. But then she picked up this box…" I stop and take deep breaths to loosen the tight band of pain across my chest. They aren't sobs, though. Never sobs.

Natalie urges me on. "Describe the box, Tom. Picture it and give us the most accurate description you can."

I continue, forcing myself to observe the memory instead of live in it, teasing out the details of the box. "It was about six inches long and four wide. Made of clay, painted. But the paint was faded, old looking. On the lid, there were three of the Egyptian symbols Eunice taught me: life, death, and rebirth. It may have been sealed around the seam with wax. It looked waxy, at least. A little shiny where the lid and the box met."

Natalie nods her head. "Good. I'll need you to help me draw a picture of that later. For now, keep going."

I do as she says. It's helping me get clearer on what happened, and I'm going to need that. "I didn't feel right about it, and I wanted her to put it down. I'd been standing on the top stair, and just as I stepped up to the landing, she read the words from the lid. She shouldn't have known the translations. I'm sure Eunice never taught her hieroglyphs like she'd taught me. So when she read them so clearly in English, it was off, wrong. And I knew, I just knew..."

My chest constricts again, but I continue. "And suddenly she changed, she held herself like her grandmother did—moved like her." I take a long, deep breath. "And when she spoke, she had that crisp Eunice way of speaking. You know what I mean? How Eunice exaggerated her accent to sound more Bostonian, more upper class?"

Natalie rolls her eyes. "Yes, we know. What did she say to you?"

"She asked me if I'd been making time with Cassie. She didn't seem to know for sure that Cassie and I were together. She sounded curious instead of the way she'd make an accusation. And then she used my shift words, and..."

I'm trapped in silence by my memory of the moment when the kind, loving young woman who helped me become a man again is suddenly inhabited by the hag I'd thought I'd escaped forever, turning me into an animal again, a slave, not at man.

I bring my fists to my forehead and close my eyes tight. I'll never be able to shove that moment from my brain. "Damn her! Damn her to hell!" I raise my eyes back to Nat's. "I didn't stick around after that. I got Cat moving as soon as his body would obey. Because I knew if I waited too long, I'd never leave that house as a man again."

I feel Gillan's hand on mine, reassuring me. "You did right, Tom. You couldn't have helped by staying and being trapped."

I don't feel reassured. I feel like I've abandoned my girlfriend to a terrible fate.

I look at the three of them. "Have any of you ever heard of magic like this?"

Gillian and Natalie shake their heads right away. Robert looks thoughtful for a moment, and then says, "Whatever she is, she isn't a skinwalker. They died out. There hasn't been any record of them in hundreds of years. Even if some survived, they can only move from body to body. They don't sit in a box and wait for a host. That's a good thing—they were nasty creatures. This sounds more like an old-fashioned possession. But as far as we know, Eunice wasn't a demon. I mean, we grew up together. She was a controlled but otherwise very normal girl."

Gillian's hand flinches away as I raise mine to bring it down hard on the table. The poker chips jump like fish in a pond. "If anyone could be called a demon, Eunice could! But don't tell me what it isn't. Tell me what it is. Tell me how I can save Cass."

The others don't react. Robert's still unruffled, Natalie's look is still curious. She asks, "Done now?"

I nod, reluctant, as I reel my temper in.

"Good boy." She pats my hand. "Robert, do you have anything in that library of yours that might help?"

"I have some older volumes on demonology, including some I picked up the last time I was in Europe and haven't had time to catalog yet. The usual arcane topics. They'd certainly discuss possession. But I don't know if there's anything there that will help. And a couple of them are in French."

"I read French," Gillian says. "I could get stuck in to those if the rest of you work on the others."

They're so civilized and scholarly. So calm. "Books? I don't need books. I need magic, I need fire, I need lightning. I need an enchanted tire iron to pry her out of there and get Cassie back."

Natalie gives me a withering look. "You said you were done."

She pauses, looking at me pointedly before she continues. "Nothing is going to get resolved tonight. It's too late in the evening, and it's too dangerous to try anything before we know what we're up against. And, my boy, this trio is old, and I'd hazard a guess, just a little drunk. I say we meet at Robert's tomorrow morning to start on those books."

"No, we should get moving. Do you expect me to just sit and wait?"

"Yes. Because Nat's right," Gillian says. "And you need to keep your head down so Eunice doesn't find out you're not dependent on anyone else to control your shifting now. If you go dashing about in anger, you'll slip up, and she'll find out fast enough. Let her think nothing has changed for you and Cat."

"You're right. I know you're right. If she doesn't know what happened after she died, that's one trick I've still got up my furry black sleeve." I take a deep breath through gritted teeth. Eunice won't control me again. "Gilly, can I stay with you? I've got nowhere to go."

"Not a good idea. If Eunice figures out you can control your form, I'd be the first person she thinks of. You'd be better off with someone else. Robert?"

Robert nods. "You can stay at the house. Plenty of room. Kevin and I still haven't mended our fences, so you won't be in danger of his finding you there." He's talking about his son who Cassie and I ratted out for using magic to peep into women's windows.

No one really has to say it, but they all know there was something more. In fact, I'm sure he murdered Eunice even though I'd never be able to prove it. But if he did, she allowed it. It's clear now she knew she wasn't going to stay dead.

I don't respond right away as I roll Robert's offer around in my head. I've never trusted him, and I've never liked him because of our unfortunate romantic rivalry for Eunice all those years ago, but he's turned out to be a stand-up guy, throwing his support behind Cassie against his own son. He even made it impossible for Kevin to handle spelled objects, including creating the potions he was so fond of, to assure that he can't use magic to hurt or manipulate people anymore.

When I don't respond right away, Natalie does a Mae West thing with her shoulder and says, "I'd be happy to loan you a room. Maybe I could even get that strip show, eh?"

I turn immediately to Robert. "Thanks, Robert. I appreciate it. Do you have a ground floor room so Cat can get in and out easily?"

"Absolutely. I have the perfect one."

I shift and hop into Gilly's bag as Cat, then she follows Robert out to his car, where I disembark and crawl under the front seat for the ride. I take no chances. Eunice isn't going to know a thing about me until the day—and it's coming soon—that I tear her out of the body she had no right to take and send her back to hell.

***

Robert settles me in to a large room on the first floor. Big windows. I crack one of them open, and the night noises waft in.

My mind races, and it doesn't want anything to do with the demands of my exhausted body. The open window beckons into the night. I start moving even as I shift, my appendages truncating, compacting smaller and smaller.

It's an easy leap to the sill. And then a short hop down to run swift and free down the drive and into the dimly lit streets of Robert's toney neighborhood, heading downtown.

Across the street from Cat's Magical Shoppe there's a bakery, and next to it, an alley. I blend in to the dark.

I watch as a shadow crosses the lace curtains on the second floor of the old Victorian that houses the shop and living quarters above it, and then the lights go out.

There isn't much to see.

There isn't much to do.

There's too damn much to feel.

I'm glad that cats can't cry. I would drown here in this alley. But even as I sit and stare at the darkened window, a plan is beginning to take shape.

A POET ONCE SAID that hope is the thing with feathers. If you buy that, then you'll believe it when I tell you that hope will hang around your feet being chummy, cooing, and waiting for bread crumbs. Just don't ever drop your guard.

Because hope, I've discovered, is also the thing with a sharp beak. Just when you're cruising comfortably close to the thing you most desire, hope will zoom right in and peck your eyes out.

Cat would normally be awake and alert long before anything gets close enough to land a peck, but he doesn't jolt to consciousness until the pigeon's beak hooks an ear and reels it in. Eunice must have a hand in this, must be sending me a message. The pain is fierce. By the time I spring to my feet with a long hisssssss, forcing cat's hackles and tail straight up, the bird is already winging away.

It lands on the bench across the street in front of the magic shop and struts along its length, peering here and there with its head rocking side to side in that irritating pigeon way. Probably looking for another victim in the dawn's new light.

It won't be me again. I haven't figured anything out here that I couldn't have figured out in a warm bed at Robert's. Staying longer isn't going to make a difference. It won't save Cassie. It won't bring her back to me.

I take one last look at the second floor, hoping to catch a glimpse of her, and I'm sure I see the gauze curtain move. I imagine her smiling down at me with only my loving girlfriend there instead of Eunice lurking behind her eyes. But Cassie doesn't brush the curtains aside. And even if she did, I know the truth. It will take more than hope to free her.

I slip out the back of the alley. Soon, I'm into the woods where some poor woodland creature will pay the price for my pain.

***

"Did you sleep at all, Tom?" Gillian asks as I enter the kitchen dressed in the clothes someone had thoughtfully placed on a chair in my room. They're a snug fit, but the length is good. And way too button-down for my taste. Must be hand-me-downs from my host.

Back when we were rivals and Robert still had hair, he looked just as good in a pair of bell-bottoms as I did, even though his were the young Republican version. And I have to admit, he always had more sense. He dropped Eunice and ran when I was still sniffing around her every chance I got. I may still have my hair and my youth, but the only other thing of value I've had in the past forty-five years was my short time with Cassie.

Gillian reaches for a gooey cinnamon roll and my stomach rumbles, responding to the empty feeling that I know food won't completely fill.

I sit down and grab for one while Robert maneuvers his way around the massive metal kitchen island, then pours me a cup of coffee from a french press. I gesture toward my clothes as he sets it down in front of me. "Thanks for these."

"Not a problem. Whatever you need while you're here, just ask." The doorbell sounds. "That'll be Natalie. Pour her a cup of coffee, would you, Gillian?" Robert heads for the door.

I'm kind of surprised he doesn't have a butler in this old mansion. I'm also surprised that he brews his own coffee. But it's early. Maybe the help hasn't arrived yet. Or maybe I don't really know anything about him because I was too busy thinking with my nether parts back in the day.

I start on my own coffee as Gillian readies

another cup. My early-morning face must be grim. She says, "If I could have kept my eyes open last night, I'd have been willing to start figuring this out right then. You're not the only one who loves Cassie, Tom."

I squeeze my eyes shut tight. I never did tell Cassie that I love her. It's too early; it's too new between us. We're both so screwed up by Eunice. But now, I wish I'd said it despite my fears when we were dozing together that last morning. She turned to smile at me, radiant, her long brown hair spilling across the bed in shining waves. But I couldn't shape my lips around the right sounds. It came out instead as "you're beautiful," while I moved toward her with only my lust letting it all hang out.

Stupid me. Always ready for action. Never ready to tell anyone what I feel. But I guess I still don't really believe that someone so good, someone so kind, could find something worthwhile in me after all those years I served, however reluctantly, on the side of evil. Even now, clenched lids keep my emotions from overflowing.

"Oh, Tom…" Gilly hugs me around the neck. "You've got the three most powerful witches on the eastern seaboard at your disposal until we have Cassie back with us. And every single one of us is happy to take our shot at destroying Eunice for good, even if we all have different reasons."

"I know," I say, unclenching, back under control, no emotions spilled. But it's been so long since I had to deal with human emotions on a daily basis. All of it, the anger, the caring, the fear, the urgency, the heartache: I don't know how to deal with any of it. Most of that just went away all those years I was Cat.

Natalie and Robert appear in the doorway, Natalie holding daintily to Robert's crooked arm. She gives Gillian a smile, but it looks more smug than friendly. "We're heading to the library now."

Gilly grabs her coffee in one hand, the cup she fixed for Nat in the other, and follows after them. I get up to go, too, my coffee forgotten, my heart in turmoil again as the empty room underscores the emptiness inside. All I want is Cassie in my arms again. I grab a pad and paper off the table as I follow Gilly down the hall. It's time to write down the plan that started forming in my Cat-brain last night.

***

Nat slams her book shut with a thud. I look up from my nap-invoking tome about Middle Eastern conceptions of the underworld, glad for a chance to do anything else with my eyes other than keep reading. I've been going back and forth between it and my plan, which now has a lot of scribbles about things to try: some of them are even sensible, but none of them are doable without knowing what will happen to Cassie if we go after Eunice.

"There's nothing in here. Not even a mention of those skinwalkers you talked about, Robert. How do we even know Cassie is still present, still there?"

"Natalie!" Gillian responds. "Of course she is! And it's just a matter of time before we figure out how to help her. We've only been working at this for a few hours."

"No, I want proof. I need to know we can still save her. If we can't, then we can just go nuclear on the old witch."

I set my book aside, "Fine. If it gets things moving, how do you prove it?"

Nat glances toward the ceiling, lips compressed. You can almost see the wheels turning. When she looks back, she points to the group with the long, sharp, red-painted nail of her left index finger. "We'd have to keep the spell we do small. We don't want a lot of magic floating around so close to Eunice. She might sense it, know we're probing. So, nothing fancy. No floating medallions or group chants like the ones we used to find Tom when he went missing."

I'm sick of this—she's acting like it's an intellectual exercise instead of life or death. Where is everyone's sense of urgency? I blurt, "So, go ahead. Tell us the plan. Let's get going."

"Tsk. Patience." Natalie gives me a scolding look. "It wouldn't put as much magic out there to use caraway and rosemary instead of invoking the Goddess."

Gillian nods. "It also has less chance of success. That's why we went all out for Tom."

"I know," Nat says. "But you forget that we already know where Cassie is, *if* she is. I've got an oil that would work well for this. All we need is for the oil to turn blue during the questing. If it does, we know it's found the backwash from her essence. We don't have to spill the oil to make the path to lead us to her. We can end the spell and reuse that little bit of essence to hide Tom from the same kind of tricks."

"So, you could find Cassie? And then you could make sure Eunice can't locate me? Let's do it." I spring up to give her a hug, but I unhug her and step back fast when she gives my butt a pinch. She's such an old pervert. And I'm trusting her with Cassie's safety? She cackles a little as I pull away. Seriously, she cackles.

"Of course it will, dear. I'm surprised you still doubt me after all I've done for you. Robert, do you have caraway, rosemary, and jasmine oil?"

"All but the jasmine oil. The rest is in the kitchen."

Gilly speaks up. "I haven't got any, either, but it's available in the shop. I could go pick some up."

I add to the plan when I realize her trip can serve a double purpose. "And you could sound out Eunice to see if she really doesn't know what went on when she was dead. If she knows how things are, then I don't have to sneak around anymore. We can be more direct, because she'll already be on the lookout for me," I say. "It's a good idea. I'm going with you." I jump to my feet, ready to take off.

"And how would that work?" Gillian asks.

"As cat. In your purse. It's huge. He'll be fine there. In a pinch, I could probably crawl in there without shifting first."

She ignores my grin.

"Don't be thick, Tom. What if she sees you?"

"I'm not letting you go near her alone."

"I don't know that you have anything to say about it. But I'm not worried for you—I'm protecting me. If you can promise me it won't mark me for trouble, you can come. But you've said you think Eunice can sense when you're near. If she can…"

"Oh hell." My grin fades. "I wasn't thinking. No, you're right. I'd only endanger you." I sit back down, adrenalin still revving and looking for a place to go. No way am I going to be able to stick my head back into a book.

"Plus, I have errands I have to run this afternoon, so I can fit all of that in before I return this evening. I'm assuming the ritual is an evening affair, Nat?"

"Absolutely, fall of darkness, all of that. Back by dusk? Would that work for everyone?"

I realize I'm clenching my fist in frustration. "We can't do this faster?"

"You want powerful magic, don't you? That

doesn't happen in minutes."

Gillian gives me a look that says she agrees, but it's a look full of sadness for me. And pity. I'm sure I see pity. Then she's out the door.

Nat and Robert sink back into their big chairs with their books full of dusty old knowledge. I try to focus, but I'm no help. I'm not a scholar, and I never was much of a warlock. Ask me to recite poetry, and I can go for hours—poetry works great on the chicks. Put on a chef's hat and make a feast? That I can do. But wrestle with what's in a witch's grimoire? No, that talent always belonged to the women around me. I'd have been helpless against a witch even when I could access my magic.

But I don't need magic now. We have the start of a plan. And I'm going to make sure that every bit of it gets explored as quickly as possible.

CASSIE'S BODY FITS ME like a glove, but didn't I pick her for that?

For long years, I enjoyed my Eunice-face, and the one I see when I look in the mirror today is close enough to feel familiar. The blue eyes, the chestnut hair, the delicate nose. It's much improved now that my fierce intelligence lights up her eyes instead of the semi-matte sheen of the girl's dull obedience.

Her wardrobe is a mess. Nothing worth wearing—every item is an off-the-rack nightmare. What did she do with my clothes? And exactly how long have I been gone? I doubt much time has passed, but my loving granddaughter appears to have obliterated me from just about everywhere in my house except the attic. I'd have expected her granddaughter to hang on to Eunice's things for a good long time, wringing her hands and sobbing about how much she misses her granny. I'm surprised to find so much of the house has been cleared of my influence.

It's simply irritating not to have kept control of the situation just because I was dead.

At least when I feel around for her in here, there's no push-back like there was with that Eunice. She had far too much influence over me, constraining me with her courtesy and civility and niceness. This girl will stay beat down where she belongs. All those years I trained her to subjugate her own will to mine appears to have worked out just fine.

I think I'll take my new body out for a walk. With the old one's creaky knees, it's been years since I could appreciate a chill night under the moon. It was late April when my spirit was gathered to my Ab Khr to wait for Cassie to release me. I could ring time and weather and find the date easily, but I can also tell from the sky.

The streetlights obscure a full view of the stars, but what I see tells me I haven't waited in that attic long. It's summer. And the cafe still has its "New Menu" sign out with the same year listed as when I left. I haven't been gone long at all.

I enjoy the breeze on my newly smooth skin. It's good to be alive in a new world ripe for the taking.

Or at least the same old world with a brand new me.

Tom won't have gone far. He never does. As I walk past the silent shops in downtown Giles, I hear rustling in the alleys from time to time and wait for him to emerge from the shadows repentant. He doesn't. But he will.

It must have been a surprise for him, expecting boring Cassie and encountering me instead. I enjoyed his look of shock and recognition.

He wasn't a cat when I returned, so Cassie must have discovered the magic words. I have to assume they had some fun after she freed him. It's his nature, my tomcat Tom. I did, after all, find myself dressed in one of the girl's nightgowns when I surfaced, with Tom in only pajama bottoms where he stood on the stairs. I would have loved to have seen the look on her insipid face when Tom first came bursting out of my kitten. It had to have been quite something.

Oh well, it's so limiting when you're dead. You miss things. And Tom will come back to me in no time. He leaves, but he always returns. In the end, he misses me.

I look forward to the improved fun factor with my new, young, juicy body. It's already humming with anticipation.

Oh my, the things we'll do.

***

My morning stretch is luxurious and completely unaccompanied by a crick in the neck, sciatica, and that grabbing feeling in my bowel. I adore this body I've stolen. I run my hands over its smooth, firm hips and abdomen. Yes, very nice. And that tingle…

Wait, that's the tingle of Cat's spell, the thread that tells me Tom is near. I certainly hope he's come home.

I slip on a nightie and focus on the direction of the magic spark. To the front of the house I go, but Tom isn't in the upstairs parlor in his basket. I realize the tingle is coming from outside. I look out to see if I can locate him, and there in the alley across the street, Cat lies curled up in the shadows, sleeping.

I'll wake him up soon enough. Maybe he'd enjoy a visit from that pigeon he's obsessed with. I look down. Yes, there it is, sitting on the bench where it spends the day waiting for the crumbs people drop after visiting the bakery.

Pigeons have such tiny brains. So easy to control, even from this distance. And with the sharp eyes I have now, I'll be able to see the entire thing in detail. How lovely. Cat really should have come home sooner. If he had, I wouldn't be forced to take drastic measures to get his attention.

I send silvery strands of magic toward the strutting bird with my wishes embedded in them. They slip under its feathers and do their work.

The pigeon flies true and drops to the ground

next to Cat without waking him. Then it reaches out and gets its beak into the papery thin flesh of kitten-Tom's ear. These eyes are so good I swear I can even see a bright bead of blood left in the nick when the pigeon pulls away. It flies back to the bench with a fuzzy triangle of skin still held in its beak before it gobbles it down upon alighting.

Cat startled awake when it happened, watched the pigeon's flight, then turned and ran out the back of the alley—the wrong way entirely. Still playing coy.

Poor Tom. Poor, bad Tom. I have so many ways to punish him when he finally slinks home.

THAT ANNOYING GILLIAN FLOUNCES through the door, accompanied by the tinkle of the shop bell. Dressed like a nightmare, as usual. Always was. She's all big, floppy bosom under loose blouses and flowing skirts, with her long white hair pinned up in a sloppy bun. I can't imagine what Tom saw in her.

"Hello sweetie," she calls to me. "Where's that cat of yours today? I've brought him a treat." She tears the top off a bag of cat snacks that smell strongly of rotting fish and walks around a set of shelves, peering into all the places a cat could hide. "Come on, Cat, I've got something special for you. It's been weeks since I've come to visit. You must have grown."

I try to fake Cassie's friendly expression, but I don't know how to work facial muscles in that direction. I do the best I can, but it feels wrong, and I don't like it in the least. "Cat stayed out all night. Not here, I'm afraid. How are you today?" I say, but I'm begging silently to be saved from having to hear her answer. I'd rather tear the girl's ears off than engage in pleasantries with this one.

"Too bad. I wanted to see how he likes these new treats. They were on special, and I immediately thought of him."

I try for a cute, girlish titter, but I only manage something that sounds suspiciously like a bird call. Faking Cassie isn't as easy as I thought it would be. Perhaps I should have observed her more closely over the years. Too late now. "Gilly, you're too nice! I'm sure he'd love it if he were here. I expect him any minute. You know Cat—he always comes back. The shop is never without a Cat for long."

"I'm sure you're right. I'll keep them in my purse for next time." She puts the packet of treats away and walks into the herb section. "I'll just pick up my shisandra and some jasmine oil then." She takes a small packet of herbs from the shelf and turns it over to look at the sticker. She always goes right to the price. How predictable.

"Goodness, Cassie! What happened? The price has nearly doubled!"

"Rising costs, Gilly. Rising costs." Of course, there are no rising costs. I've simply repaired some of the damage Cassie did to the prices while I was gone. There's no competition in Giles for what

Cat's Magical Shoppe supplies, and there are a large number of witches and new age-y tourists who want it. Dropping prices under those conditions just isn't good business.

"Oh, it's terrible, isn't it?" she agrees. "Prices just go up and up and up. I imagine the small business owner has a hard time these days."

I expect a fight from her. She would have fought with Eunice. I always enjoyed the conflict, along with her inability to let go of Tom—I could just bring that up, and she'd be off in a frenzy of outrage. It was easy for me to take him away, of course, but I still enjoyed having deprived her. I can't poke that wound as Cassie. It will be difficult, but not impossible, to keep Gillian roughed up about that rivalry. I'll need to find a creative approach to the subject.

I smile brightly at her. Once again, that doesn't feel like the right response, but I have no idea what emotion the girl would show or how she'd show it. She was always perky, always chirpy. That or sobbing about some ridiculous thing she'd blown up in her mind to be a tragedy. I haven't prepped for anything else. "Oh yes, the small business owner is really in a bind. Can I ring that up for you?"

"Absolutely." She hands me her selections, and I check the prices as though I hadn't just written them up myself this morning. "That comes to twelve eighty-three with tax."

As she hands me a twenty and I make change,

she asks, "Have you decided if you're going to be there next week, Cass?"

"What's that?"

"Choir practice?"

I cover for myself, not knowing that the coven would be meeting before the full moon, which I did mark on the calendar once I'd pinned down the date of my return. Or that Cassie even knew about the choir. But with the skills I taught her without her knowledge, it isn't surprising she would be attracted to the opportunity if it was offered. "Oh yes, of course. In Corey Woods, right?"

"Yes. Just a quick one. A cleansing. We'll gather just before midnight. Nat tells me that Janice has been feeling unbalanced and needs to get back to a good place. She doesn't want to wait for the next full moon because her magic has been so unreliable lately. "

"That'll be nice," I say. But oh, that'll be boring. Let's raise some demons instead. I've got old friends I want to see.

"See you then, sweetheart."

After she leaves, I try to remember all of the items she buys regularly as I busy myself with the pricing marker.

***

Why is the shop so busy? It seems like everyone in town comes by and lingers. It's maddening. I had a steady trade built up, but they got in and out: it was nothing like this. I hate it. That girl has them all coming in to browse and socialize. They feared me, but they needed what I could provide. In a very short time of being nice to people, she's ruined a lifetime of building the shop's reputation.

It takes me hours to familiarize myself with what's been rearranged. It's difficult to manage in-between the far too frequent interruptions by townsfolk wanting a chin-wag. Eventually, I find the latest Archeology Today magazine shoved under the counter unread. I pull up the stool and start paging through it, relishing the familiar names from my past.

And then—wait...a team has discovered a previously unknown tomb. Have they found him? My hopes rise each time someone digs deep beneath the Egyptian sands, but it always comes to naught.

I read quickly, consumed by the notes about the discovery. And then, there it is—the picture from the top of the sarcophagus.

I know that face.

I can't breathe. Is my heart still beating? Yes, it is. It is. I take in a long, glorious breath with my young lungs and the burst of oxygen tingles all the way to my toes.

Finally, after all these years of waiting. I spring into action.

"Out! Out! The shop is closing early!" Two teenage girls dressed in black look at me like I'm deranged, but I've never felt saner. A murderous glance has them running for the exit soon enough.

It takes me half an hour to book a flight, hotel, and cab. It takes somewhat longer to find Cassie's passport. Eunice's certainly won't do.

All these years waiting, moving from place to place, body to body, hoping that someone will discover through the urge of human curiosity what I have not been able to discover under the black moon, and now it's done.

ROBERT KNOCKS ON THE GUEST bathroom door where I've managed to finally grab the shower I've gone without for too long. "Gillian just phoned. She's on her way."

I head toward the kitchen as soon as I can, dressed only in jeans, still drying my hair on one of Robert's thick towels. Natalie's helping in the kitchen as they make dinner. I wish I'd remembered that and gone for a shirt before coming out.

She grins. "Stand just there, Tom. No, don't move. Yes, with the light through the window illuminating just the slightest sheen of water on that lean but muscular torso, I can see that I should have done anything in my power to sample your wares years ago. If only I'd not been so wary of what Gillian and Eunice might do. And now with Cassie in the mix, as soon as we get her back, well...I fear my time will never come."

"Not in the mood for it, Nat." I drape the towel around my shoulders like a cape. My days of chasing tail are long over, and I don't need Nat reminding me of what I used to be when my unasked-for Cat side is a more than adequate reminder on its own. "Robert, did Gilly find anything out?"

"She's got good news and bad news. She wants to give them both at once when everyone is available."

I head up the stairs to find a shirt. I normally wouldn't be bothered by Nat's teasing attentions. She's harmless enough. But I'm on edge, barely slept, and don't need any more bad news even if it's tempered with something positive.

After I'm dressed, I sit quietly while Robert and Natalie bring the meal to the dining room table. He puts on a good feed. It's amazing he's stayed so lean at his age. I can't even begin to tell them what their dedication to helping Cassie means to me. I don't think my mouth would form the words. I'm so terrible with emotion after having been Cat for most of the past forty-five years that if I started to say it, I'm afraid I'd lose it completely. It will have to go unsaid.

When Gilly bursts in the back door, she's breathing hard like she ran in from the car. "She left! Sue from the bakery told Dash, who told

Janice, that she saw Eunice leaving the shop with a suitcase."

"She's gone? Cassie's gone?" Eunice is going to tear me apart a piece at a time until there's nothing left of me. It's no coincidence Cat lost a snip of ear to that pigeon—that's just Eunice's way of letting me know that the pain will never end. I ball my fists and lower my head to the table top to keep from screaming out my rage.

"Don't panic, Tom. Don't." She hurries to me and strokes my hair. I raise my eyes, and hers are there: kind, supportive, and determined. "I checked it out, and the sign on the door says the shop will be open again on Thursday. That's only a few days. There's no reason to think she won't be back right on time. And from talking to her, I'm absolutely sure she has no knowledge of anything that happened after she died. But, yes, this alarms me, too. Can you think of anything Eunice was planning before she died that would cause her to suddenly close the shop and leave?"

In my head, I run through the last few months I spent in captivity with Eunice. "No, nothing. Business as usual. She was consumed with the same old power-mongering and vicious commentary about everyone in town." I pause as my voice catches. I take a deep breath before continuing. "Gilly, she could disappear, and we'd never find her."

Natalie clears her throat. "I think that's unlikely,

Tom. Never underestimate the witches of Giles. Gillian, do you have the jasmine oil?"

"Bloody hell, I left it out in the car. I got distracted when Janice called. Couldn't think of anything else. And I realized while I was at the shop that Tom had been working there. I covered myself by saying I hadn't been in for several weeks, but you know how everyone talks. They're bound to ask about the handsome shop clerk and when he'll be back. Eunice is going to wonder how none of us recognized him."

The corners of Nat's lips twitch up. I think she gets happier the more difficult things get. "You can dash out to the car for the oil after dinner, dear. We've got work to do. But dinner first, my busy bees. We all need to keep our strength up."

I countermand her, saying "Gilly, get it now. We can plan during dinner. A quick dinner." Natalie starts to protest, but I cut her off. "You're high priestess. I get that. I appreciate that. But this is my battle, with my enslaver, for my girlfriend's life, and we don't have time to linger over our meal. We've got a lot of problems to solve, and I'm not waiting."

She narrows her eyes, then shrugs and heads for the kitchen to start bringing in the food while Gilly heads out back to her car.

By the end of dinner, we've got a three-pronged plan that gets us closer to getting Cassie back. First, we prove Cassie is still there. I know she is, so I'm not worried. This is just to keep Nat from going after Eunice half-cocked. Second, I need to be hidden so Eunice can't trace me and find out about everyone who is helping me in the process. It's probably lucky that she's gone out of town or she would have started looking for me already.

We can't cover the fact that I worked in the store yet, but we've got some ideas about how to go about that when Eunice gets home.

Three steps closer to Cassie. We'll be ready. I know we will.

***

After I race to the kitchen with the dirty dishes and stack them in the dishwasher in record time, Natalie lays out her supplies and gets to work.

"Tom, you understand that you'll be both the possessor of the lost object in the first casting and the lost object in the second?" She stands behind me with her hands on my shoulders while Gillian lights candles all around us. The chair is plain oak. Natalie doesn't want interference from anything plastic or artificial. I think she's more of a purist than she lets on.

"I understand. Although I don't think that Cassie would like it much if I go around saying I own her."

"Technically it's not a spell for things that are lost in an ownership sense. You wouldn't use this spell to find lost coins. It's for something that you care about. Is there anything you care about more than Cassie?"

I glance at Gillian. "No. I have an old friend who stood by me even when I didn't deserve it who runs a close second, though." Okay, maybe I actually can say some of those difficult things I feel once in a while. Cassie has helped me begin to open up.

Natalie catches Gillian's return smile and snorts. "Tom, get a grip, you're flirting while I'm telling you that you need to focus?"

I shake my head and sigh. "I haven't stopped thinking about Cassie for a second since Eunice puffed out of that box like fiery demon's breath. It wouldn't be possible for me to be more focused."

"Fine, then. Let's begin." Natalie waves the others out of the room. Robert turns out the lights on his way and closes the door. We're alone in the near-darkness, lit only by three candles. Her hand on my shoulder feels heavy and warm.

"Hold your hands out. Cup them." I do as I'm told, and she places a small copper bowl with a greenish patina into them. Then, she removes the ceramic vessel that she'd hung around her neck on a cord. She leans over me to pour the contents into the bowl. "Don't turn, Tom. Continue to look ahead. Look at the reflective surface of the liquid in the bowl and try to see what you've lost there. Picture Cassie and your feeling for her."

I do as I'm told, and the oil in the copper container begins to warm. It becomes almost too hot to hold.

"Don't remove your hands," Natalie warns. "It won't burn you, I promise." I focus again, but it's difficult. With thoughts of Cassie comes pain.

Natalie bends to my ear. "Are you focused? Do you see?"

I concentrate everything that I am toward picturing Cassie—that last night together, her hair softly brushing my face as she bent down from above to kiss me.

Her face appears in the surface of the oil. Her loving face. I can't pull my eyes away from it. I barely notice that the oil is turning blue.

Then, the image is projected above the liquid, shimmering and vaguely formed. A tendril begins to grow from the side, reaching and twisting outward. It's found her. It's drawing a path.

"Now, Tom, dump it over your hair and skin. We need to cover every part of you. We've proven Cassie is still there. And we'll use that piece of her essence you've found to disguise yours."

I drop my robe and pour the oil over my head, spreading it first through my hair and then across my skin. As Natalie promised me, it doesn't burn me.

"Make sure you're thoroughly covered." At least Natalie doesn't offer to help me out. I'm finding that magic may be the one thing she takes seriously.

She circles me in the candle light, pointing. "There, more coverage. Good." In a moment, her voice comes from behind. "You've missed a spot just below your left buttock."

I can't believe she resists an off-color remark as I smooth the oil down across my backside.

She makes one more circuit. "Yes, we're done. You can put your robe back on as soon as the oil is dry to the touch. That will only take a couple of minutes. But no showering for 24 hours. You have to give the magic time to attach itself fully to your skin. If you don't, this will all be for nothing."

I grab my robe off the floor as she continues, "We'll have to skip poker tonight in favor of hide and seek. When you're dry enough, get dressed and come let us know. Our best test is to see if any of us can find you."

As it turns out, while I lay on the grass just to the side of the wooden deck off Robert's spacious back living room staring up at the limitless stars, none of the witches are able to catch a magical whiff of me. There's a little spring to my step when I come back into the house after Natalie calls out, "Ollie-ollie-oxen-free". It's not just because I won at hide and seek. Or that her call reminded me of simpler times. Mostly, my heart hasn't stopped singing since Cassie's face appeared over the bowl. She's still there. She's still mine. And I know I'm going to save her.

I even have a little plan of my own that I'm not

sharing with the team right now. They'd come up with some reason I shouldn't go ahead with it, but I'm not waiting any longer than I have to to take Cassie back from that evil witch.

***

It's nearing midnight when I explore the outside of the shop on Cat's padded feet that slide through the grass without a sound as I look for an open window. Tonight, I'm a panther. Silent, deadly, the very definition of sleek.

With my head craned upwards, I trip unexpectedly, do a head over heels roll, and look back to see that I'd stumbled over a landscaping stone that's been there for every one of Cat's lives.

Sure. Right. Tonight I'm a panther. Tiny, harmless, and prone to rolling around adorably in the tensest situations.

This little caper is starting out great.

I can't believe Eunice would go away without leaving a window cracked open for Cat. Has she given up? No, no way would she just let me go free. I can't let myself believe that for a minute. It will only make it harder when she snaps a leash onto my collar again.

I know I shouldn't think that way—Cassie would call me out on it, but I won't let myself go chasing after hope again. I have one thing to focus on: I need to find something that will help get

Cassie free. After that, it doesn't matter what happens to me.

No, if Eunice didn't remember to crack a window, she just wasn't thinking about me when she left. That can only be a good thing. The vise of anxiety I'm wearing around my chest loosens a little.

Or maybe she doesn't plan to be away as long as she said she would: as soon as I think that, my panic revs up again. It could be a trick to lure me back. She found out about me being in control of the shifting magic and figures I'd need my ID to skip town, so she pretended to go away. If she doesn't know about me and Cassie, she'd have no reason to think I'd stay.

I take a long breath. This needs to stop. I have to stop imagining scenarios that keep me running scared. There's no evidence for any of it, and even if it is a trick, my head has to be clear to fight her if she turns up.

Cat's not worried. He's more than sure he could outrun her if she popped out from behind the parlor window like some demonic jack-in-the-box. I take strength from that. He's small, but he's scrappy. I can do this. I can find that box she used against Cassie and take it back to Robert's. And the friendly neighborhood witches? They'll figure out what to do with it if I keep the pressure on. It's only a matter of time.

There's no way for Cat to get in, that's clear soon enough. I prowl to the back while I think about the best approach to the problem. I don't have tools, and if I shift, I'll be exposed, vulnerable. I'll also be locked outside in the buff.

I could go wake up Gillian to help with the locks, but I'm so close now. I don't need her trying to talk me out of it.

Unless Eunice has changed things since she returned, there's no alarm in the shop, only the video cameras to deter shoplifters. No one who lives in this town would have risked her ire by breaking in.

I shift myself, trying not to make a sound as I experience the pain that always accompanies my transformation. Then, when I'm able, I pick up that troublesome landscape rock and pitch it at the side parlor window. It shatters on the first try. I shift back to cat and leap through gracefully, careful to jump out beyond where the shards of glass are strewn.

I thought I'd leapt far enough, but a sharp pain in my left front paw tells me I misjudged. I raise the throbbing paw to take a look. A piece of the window glass pierced Cat's left front paw as it met the floor. The cut is deep and dangerous. Cat can see no reds, but the gray blood flows freely. He's in trouble.

I move a few steps farther into the house to make sure I really am out of the danger zone this time and shift again. A third shift in such a small period of time is agony, and I take longer to recover than normal. I'm completely defenseless while I try to get control over my human limbs but flail helplessly instead as the pain and the lingering sensations of Cat fade too slowly.

My heart races out of control. If Eunice walks in, it's all over.

I'M FREAKING OUT. I'm freaking out. I'm freaking out.

Cat's injury won't harm him until I shift to his form again, but he'll need medical attention immediately then, or he's done for.

I take a huge breath and blow it back out. Calmer. But still panicked.

I take another breath. And another. And another.

I have to put my fear aside and focus on one thing: Eunice has Cassie. And she's not keeping her. Not even if Cat loses his last two lives. Not even if I lose mine.

I have to get what I'm looking for and get out before anyone notices that broken window. Then I've got to get from downtown to the ritzy section of Giles where Mayor Robert lives without being stopped for indecent exposure.

Looks like I'm not going to need the pouch I put on my collar for the ID. I'm going to have to take some of my clothes from the house so I can get across town as a human, and if I do, Eunice could discover that they're gone and wonder why. That's a lot of "ifs", though. First, she would have had to go through Cassie's closets and found my stuff there. And once I take them, she'll have to go through them again to find out that they're gone.

There's a chance she'll never know. A big chance.

Really? Who am I kidding? Eunice notices everything.

No, maybe not. Gillian bought me some new, modern clothes that my former mistress has never seen. If I only take some of those, even if she did notice them, she might not realize they've disappeared or even that they belonged to me. She'd miss one of my dashikis, but she wouldn't miss a plain v-neck t-shirt. I work to make my panic subside. I need my brain back.

I find my wallet in the back pocket of my pants as I slide into them. That's a stroke of luck. I hope it means Eunice didn't find it.

Once I'm dressed, I creep quietly up the stairs, although I don't know why I feel the need for silence. There's no one here, and if there was, silence wouldn't help me. Even with Nat's cloaking spell, I'm terrified Eunice will sense me.

But she's not here. She's not here. Say it, rinse, repeat.

She's not here.

Big breath. Let it go slowly. And then one more. Continue up the stairs like a man. *You can do this for Cassie.*

I stop on the stairs before I enter the attic. The tension weighs me down. I keep flashing to the image of Cassie standing there, reading the words on the lid of the box...and then...Eunice laughing at me from Cassie's face with a promise of pain.

It's pitch black up here and smells like dust and abandonment. I grope for the string of the bulb to the left of the door. I feel like Cat, batting at invisible combatants in a beam of sunlight.

Then I find the string and tug.

Light fills the dark corners of the room. My adrenalin levels start to drop.

I walk to where Cassie found the box. There's nothing here now except a clean rectangle in the dust, a place that had been covered and now is not. Eunice moved it. But where could it be?

I open every trunk, every box of old-lady junk, careful to memorize the location of each item so that I can return it to its exact place when I'm done. I can't have Eunice knowing I've been here if I don't find what I've come for. I'd never get back in the house for a second look.

After a half hour or so, I run out of patience. It's not in the attic. I've explored every inch.

A thud, followed by the sound of footsteps downstairs, turns my frustration to fear.

***

I'm paralyzed, visualizing Eunice coming up the stairs, visualizing her preventing me from shifting myself and trapping me forever as Cat, forever separate from Cassie. Not to mention bleeding out from Cat's injury while she capers around doing a victory dance.

It's not Eunice. It can't be her. I listen for more clues.

It's a male voice—no, two male voices. I hear a riser creak as at least one of them starts up the stairs to the second floor. Then another follows.

A whisper. "It's clear." It sounds official. Sounds like the fuzz.

At least it's not Eunice. Not that I can let them find me. I'm not afraid of them—I have a right to be in this house, assuming Eunice hasn't told anyone that Cassie's new boyfriend has moved out. And with Robert's help, after what may have been unnecessary blackmail, I've got government-issued ID, too.

Still, I don't want anyone mentioning to Eunice that I was here. And how do I explain the broken window?

I strip and throw my clothes and tennis shoes behind a box, then lay on my side until I hear the officers stopping at the open door to the attic stairs. I leave the light on because turning it off now will only alert them that someone must be up here.

I think *bad Tom*, and by the time the cop's head pops over the top of the landing, following the barrel of his pistol, the only living thing that greets him is a sleeping cat. He comes all the way up the stairs, probably wondering what that light's doing on in an otherwise dark house. I pretend to wake, and he bends over to scratch beneath my chin when I give him Cat's friendly stare.

"Nobody up here but the cat. Whoever broke the window is long gone. Maybe it wasn't even a break-in. I'll get my brother-in-law out to board it up and we can sort it out with the owner when she surfaces."

When he leaves, I bring Cat's damaged paw out from underneath me where I'd kept it hidden, and the floor and my fur are slick with his blood.

I feel woozy. They're still downstairs when I shift again, but I can't wait for them to leave. Cat is losing blood way too fast. He's on his seventh life now. He's only got the two lives left, and Eunice always made it clear to me that when his last life is used up, my one life goes with it. I'm not going to waste any more of the time I have left.

I breathe a sigh of relief when they're gone, but I can't linger and search the rest of the house now. They've got someone on the way to board up the window, and I can't be here when he arrives.

Once I'm clothed, and I've mopped up every bit of Cat's blood from the attic and shoved the paper towels I used into a pocket, I get all the way to the back door before I remember the perfect thing to get me back to Robert's without being detected by the cops. I can hear them talking through the broken window, probably keeping an eye on things from outside while waiting for the brother-in-law to arrive. I may have learned a lot about stealth from Cat, but it's a lot easier for a Cat to go undetected than it is for an over-six-foot guy.

I hurry back upstairs and reach under my bed for what looks like an empty paper bag and put on Kevin's invisibility suit by feel, pulling the flap on the hood down over my face after I find it by exploring along the top of the hood with my fingers. It's filmy, but I can see out fine. I rush downstairs, dash through the back door, and make sure to lock it up on my way out.

I slip out the back and head home without fear of being spotted by the watchful eye of the police.

But heading back undetected isn't much consolation: I didn't find anything. I failed Cassie again.

***

Robert sets a cup of hot tea in front of me and takes the opposite seat at the kitchen table. Goddess knows what's in this batch of his herbal brew. It smells like a stink bug. "I'm sorry to hear you weren't successful, Tom. But why didn't you let any of us know?" He pushes the cream and sugar over on its tray. I don't think it's going to help. "If something happens to you, it won't help Cassie."

"I didn't want Gillian talking me out of it, and I know her well enough to know she would have. It's that simple." I would have preferred to regale him in the morning, but I don't have a key, and I couldn't slip in through the gap in the window without risking Cat's health. I didn't have a choice. I had to make a ruckus at the back door until I woke him up.

"Understood. But just let me in on it next time. Maybe I can help." His head moves slightly, and the light from the lamp over the table glints off his bald scalp. "Can Cat heal on his own?"

"No, when one of us is active, it's like the other one of us goes into that suspended animation all the science fiction books used to talk about. It's why I didn't age much over the years. My body was in storage a lot." I can see Robert's thinking about that, taking it in. Maybe wishing he'd had a similar arrangement for his hair. "But Cat's in storage with an injury that's going to kill him fast after he comes to if nothing gets the bleeding stopped."

"I'll get a call in to Darrin in the morning, then. You remember him? I believe he was with the choir when they gathered to free you from the shop? He's a veterinarian, which seems appropriate, as well as a fine healer on the magical side of things."

Nat must have filled him in on my recent history because no way did we ask Robert to join in on that particular ritual—I still believed he was an enemy back then. I'm not convinced he should be getting the "all clear" from me even now, but he's the coven's high priest, and Nat is the high priestess. I expect she felt she had to bring him up to speed on everything that's been going on. They spent years disliking each other, so it's odd to see them working together so well and being so friendly. It must be Cassie's influence. She does good things to people. Did good things. Oh hell, will do good things again. Guaranteed.

I'm glad Cat's going to be looked after, but it doesn't make me feel any better that I failed to get the box. The very fact that Eunice has hidden it makes me feel sure it's the key to freeing Cassie. I need to get back in there before she comes back. Once Cat's sorted, nothing's going to stop me.

THE NEXT MORNING, DARRIN works fast and efficiently. As soon as Cat's body stops juddering through the shift, he's at the paw with a hypodermic, apologizing for only being able to give a tiny amount of anesthetic due to Cat's size, and has it stitched up lickety-split, stanching the flow. Despite the painkiller, there's plenty sting while he sews.

Afterward, Cat still feels weak, but he's no longer in danger.

The doc deftly grinds the ingredients for a poultice and pours the fine powder out of the mortar over two large snakeweed leaves. Then, he arranges the whole mess on a gauze bandage and wraps Cat's foot up tight with it.

He holds his hands to his heart as he chants softly. "Wrapped in cotton, bound with care, grant this healing, and suffering forbear." Short and sweet, just the way I like my healing chants.

When he moves his hands from his heart to Cat's injury, his energy stops the rest of the pain completely. I allow Cat to get up, but he gently pushes me back down.

"The wound is going to heal quickly, but not that quickly. You need to stay off that foot for 24 hours and be careful of it for several days."

That won't work for me. I need to get back into Eunice's place before she returns home. I can't sit around being Cat. I make a loud yowl of complaint.

"I can knock you out completely if you can't follow instructions." He looks over at my host. "Robert?"

Robert looks thoughtful, but I draw the vet's attention back by patting him with my good front paw. When he looks down at me, I draw the bad one into my chest protectively, roll my head over in a way that traps an ear against the table and thrusts Cat's nose upward, and close my eyes. Despite being the only thing I could think of to communicate, I bet that move looks oh-my-god-look-how-sweet-he-is adorable. At least we're all men here and nobody gets all gooey about it.

"Good. A series of cat naps is just the thing."

Cat's all for the naps. I'm stuck. I can't risk his life for my impatience.

***

If people want me to pay attention, how could anyone think it's a good idea to make Cat comfy on a chair covered with fringed pillows? And it's that good fringe too, the long, thick stuff you find on old fabrics. I try to pay attention while the coven plans, but Cat's attention is elsewhere. There's all that swingy movement to be had with a bat and a smack and a little twitch of the unbandaged claw.

My understanding of the meeting is all just "we need to decide if we should"...swap, swip, swish..."but we don't know"...fweep, fwap, shake..."well, a cleansing never really goes amiss"...flop, roll, grab...

Natalie's voice rises above the quieter ones. "Bats on a biscuit! Someone *please* do something about that cat."

That gets my attention. From my upside down position, I look over and she's glaring meaningfully at Gillian. Like I'm anyone's responsibility but my own.

I don't mind taking my new seat constrained against Gillian's shoulder. It's much easier to follow things now. Too bad the meeting's breaking up.

I'm going to need to read someone's notes just in case there's a quiz later.

As everyone gets up to leave, Gillian calls to Darrin, "Could you stay a bit longer? I've a favor to ask."

"Of course." He ambles over. I've got my own chair now that Cat no longer needs to be on lock down. Gillian slides a pen and piece of paper his way.

She says, "You recall we discussed how we're going to cover ourselves if Eunice discovers Tom has been working in the shop and many of us would have seen him?"

"Absolutely, the fake Tom quitting in a huff because the shop is closed? It's a great plan."

"Have you ever given Eunice anything in writing?"

"Can't say as I have...oh, I see. You need someone to write the letter!"

"Yes, someone with a masculine hand. I expect she's had letters from both Tom and Robert and could obviously recognize their writing."

"Happy to, happy to. What would you like me to say?" He picks up the pen and poises it over the paper.

"Just that you're resigning from the position because you're tired of expecting to work and finding the shop closed instead. Also that you've left your name tag and dropped your keys through the letter flap on your way out. Something like that. Then sign it 'Tom Collins' to match the name tag we've prepared."

Darrin busies himself with the letter, and Gillian looks it over when he's done.

"That's perfect. What do you think of yourself, then?" She pulls out a plastic photo name tag and hands it to him.

"Well, well, you did a nice job with that. They do look a lot alike, don't they? Just enough that if someone describes our Tom, the description would also fit this young man."

I poke my head up and take a gander at the guy in the picture. Kind of squinty. Big nose. I don't see the resemblance. He's nowhere near as good-looking as I am.

They make their goodbyes, then Gillian takes her copies of the shop keys out of her bag and places them and the name tag into a pocket. She chucks me under the chin before she leaves. "Well, that's ready to go. I'm on my way to the shop, so wish me luck."

I would wish her luck, or at least walk her to the door, but Cat suddenly remembers that there's fringe just a quick leap away.

***

The next morning, Darrin stops by and checks his handiwork. He gives Cat a clean bill of health with a warning to take it easy until the paw is fully healed, so I shift immediately.

As soon as I'm able, I grab the jeans and shirt Robert laid out for me and get Darrin moving toward the door. "Thanks, doc, really. I owe you," I say, as I steer him along toward the front door with a friendly hand on the back. He snags his bag as he goes.

"Watching you transform is mesmerizing."

"Yeah, yeah, mesmerizing. In a totally not-at-all-weird, we're-all-manly-men kind of way, right? Thanks again." I close the door in his face before he has a chance to burst into song about my painful transformation habit.

I turn and rush back to the study where Robert has his head buried in a book.

"Fill me in. Right now. What did you guys plan while I was suffering from cat brain? I know about the fake Tom, but what else?"

He holds up a finger and continues reading for a moment, then places an embossed leather bookmark and closes the book. "You didn't hear the entire thing?"

"Somebody put a cat on a chair full of fringed pillows. How much do you think I heard?"

Robert smiles at that. "I see. Then, yes, let's talk."

He leans back and holds his interlaced hands against his mouth for a moment before he begins. "Natalie is going to put Eunice to sleep in hopes that Cassie will then be in control again."

"She can do that?"

"She thinks so. And I believe she can." He inclines his head toward me, "Keep this between you and me, if you could, but I've always thought Natalie was an extremely accomplished caster. Despite our differences through the years, I admire her abilities. She's really quite a witch."

"I definitely won't pass that on. Because how long would we have to listen to her brag on and on about being a master caster after that, do you think?"

Robert returns my grin. "Two, three years, maybe?"

"In that range," I agree. "But she can just put her to sleep, and we'll have Cassie back? Just like that?"

His grin fades. He shakes his head. "I'm sorry, Tom. It's not that simple. Natalie wants to talk to Cassie, but she can't keep Eunice asleep forever. It won't be very long. Maybe half an hour, maybe minutes. There aren't that many coven members we know we can trust, and the fewer people involved, the less oomph behind the spell."

"It's not good enough, damn it! What good is all this magic if it won't help me save her? What good is any of it?"

He stands and moves to place a hand on my shoulder, but I shrug it off. "Leave me alone."

"You'll get to talk to her, Tom. It's more than I got when my wife died. I don't mean to be a downer, but I would have given anything to have just a few minutes with her to tell her one last time how I feel."

"I'm not losing her, so don't even talk like that. How can you be giving up like this?" I feel my face growing hot, my anger starting to boil.

"We're not giving up. I'm just saying…"

"And I'm just not listening." I storm to my room and shed my human body. Cat is going hunting, sore paw and all.

A WELL-CHOSEN SPELL SENDS the guards at the tomb's open mouth walking away into the desert accompanied by my driver. I'll have no trouble finding my way back to Cairo in the stolen cab. By the time they come to themselves with no memory of how they'd gotten there, they'll be well on their way to death by dehydration. The sands are dangerous with no place to escape the sun and no compass to point the direction home.

I can't have them describing me after I've gone, can I? Not with what I've come to do. Grave-robbing is endemic with the political upheaval in Egypt, but no one would let me just walk away with what I plan to take.

The desert air cleaves to me in a hot embrace. It's been too long. I've waited thousands of years.

I've worn hundreds of bodies, some better than this one, some worse. And yet I never stopped believing this time would come.

As I go deeper into the tomb, I need light. I blow across the girl's palm and a cool flame starts there, inches above and not burning, only illuminating. I take my time as I read the hieroglyphs along the way. Usually, there would be stories of the bravery and leadership of pharaohs, but here there is no human braggadocio to interrupt the stories of gods and goddesses. All of the paintings celebrate the power of Ba'al and his sister wives. It's promising. Very promising. But all the small openings lead to side chambers which contain only uninteresting artifacts, not the main attraction.

The passage ends, but it's clear it continues on beyond the massive stone that blocks it. The stone block cuts the story-telling in half, one arm and one leg of a figure showing at the seam with the rest behind.

It's not much of an impediment for me. I assume the diggers planned explosives for it. They won't be needed when I'm done: I hope they appreciate the favor. The government can have most of what's behind this curtain. I am here for only one thing.

The stone crumbles when I lay my hands on it. The gravel moves off down the corridor behind me with only a little effort of my will, but I make sure to leave a smooth path by which I can leave easily.

I've entered similar chambers before and found myself misled, taken in by the ones who came after, who called themselves Ba'al to impress their local tribes and claim Ba'al's strength. But there is only one Ba'al, my Ba'al, the first to be called Master.

I grew tired through the centuries of being lured to Egypt when I caught a scrap of news that turned out to lead to a pretender. It took so long to travel in those days, only to discover they'd unearthed some small, local deity, many of whom were even human. Ridiculous! Pretenders to the throne who confused the historians.

This time, no one has claimed it to be his tomb. But I saw the writing on the wall, as they say. The style of the tomb paintings and their subject matter was enough to tell me I had to see it for myself. It's only a hundred miles or so from where I last saw him. A hundred miles was a long distance in those ancient times, but it was not so far for a god.

The corridor opens into the burial chamber now. The air is poor in here, but I won't be staying long. I take frequent, deep draws of it to satisfy the needs of this body.

The sarcophagus is undisturbed. It's remarkable no tomb robber has found it. It looks exactly as it would if it had been sealed yesterday. The canopic jars that look so much like the knock-offs I lined up around the top of the shop are placed just so, the organs inside still waiting for renewed use in the afterlife.

I walk to the coffin and run my fingers across the smooth lid, reading the words as much with my fingertips as with my eyes. The painted face is the face I knew. It's him. It's Ba'al.

I lift the heavy lid with magic, although I would sacrifice these arms, this back, these legs gladly if I had to. His remains are still wrapped in decaying folds of cloth. The mummy smells of antiquity and dust. I picture him beneath the cloth as he must be now. In such a well-preserved tomb, he might even still be recognizable.

But I haven't come to admire a corpse.

I set the clay Ab Khr that I prepared so many years ago beside me on the ground. I stabilize my mind around one thought and then extend my hand toward the mummy's chest and sink it deep, tearing through the rotted cloth and dried out flesh below the rib cage. When I pull it out again, I cradle his heart in my palm, then raise it to my lips for a kiss.

I kneel to place it into the Ab Khr and close the lid, sealing it with the beeswax and herbal potion that is traditional to my people. I murmur my intent to gather his essence back from the universe. Although there can be no breeze in this underground stone chamber, a soft draft moves my hair.

I close the box and my own heart nearly bursts with joy. It wells within me like lava flowing up from the heart of a volcano. It is hot and abundant, and it will burn away anything that gets in its way.

He has been gone so long it will require strong magic to draw him back to me. It's time to go home and get back *everything* I've lost.

***

It should have been an exhausting flight. I barely notice, I'm so buoyed up by my precious cargo. Getting through customs with a mummy's heart should be difficult, even impossible. But for me, I'm sure it will just be an amusing stroll. And if it isn't? I have a backup plan.

I keep the Ab Khr close, hidden in a large handbag my Eunice persona would reject as something Gillian would buy. It pulls my entire silhouette down. But until Ba'al has eyes to go with his heart, it makes no difference.

I hope he'll be pleased with my choice. He would have liked Eunice better—her extreme lean body was so much like my original one. It seems unfair that I could choose a form for him that pleases me when he has no choice in mine. Of course, he can choose any body for me on his return, and I will happily let go of this one to please him. But the small amount of wealth and property I've accrued could be lost, and those things are not so easy to gain in a world that doesn't leave gifts at our altars. It's no fortune, but it's enough for us to be comfortable anywhere we choose.

Once Ba'al takes Tom's body, he can easily

override the human personality, destroying it and taking the Cat magic for his own. There was so little passed through history about his love of sneaking around in his alternate form, but the interest in cats you see in so many tombs was attributable to the cat-shifting god.

As I approach customs, I gaze casually at each of the officers in turn, blinking in a lazy way and yawning. As I do, each of them grows tired, asleep on his or her feet in seconds. I pass as they snooze. When they awake, they will be unaware that they had done anything more than blink.

The other sheep just wait for the attention of the officers to return. It won't surprise me if they start bleating.

I don't count on the armed guard on the other side of the customs tables who sees me pass unquestioned. I yawn, but he remains alert. Not suggestible. None of that useful human empathy. I've never had patience for his kind unless I needed a killer within easy reach.

As he heads for the end of the tables with his eyes on me, I reach for my middle, then snatch and twist the fine chain around my waist to break it and activate the spell I'd earlier cast in preparation for just this possibility. He falls with a snapped neck.

I drop the broken chain in a trash can on my way out.

SEE? THIS IS WHAT HAPPENS when you're nice to the common people. They break your windows when they're not rifling through your tombs. The note I find on the downstairs parlor table tells me that the window is boarded due to a possible break-in. Then it asks me to drop everything to let the police know I'm okay. Like it's their business where I go or what I do. How has Kevin let them get so out of control? He's a simpering little toady, but he certainly had his uses when it came to keeping the local police force leashed.

I pick up the second note. Oh, how nice. The bill for boarding up the window. And an offer to repair it with a 10% discount to boot.

This all wouldn't have been such a surprise if I hadn't packed Eunice's cell phone instead of

Cassie's on sheer force of habit. I snatch hers from the counter, and there are several messages. Most of them are from the police to tell me about the broken window and remind me to call when I can. One is from that awful Dan whom Cassie was engaged to, begging her to reconsider their relationship, and another is from Gillian reminding me about "choir practice" tonight.

I have no interest in attending, but I'll have need of the coven soon, so I can't blow my cover just yet. "Cassie" will have to attend. But I still have time to try to figure out who was here and what they wanted.

Nothing appears to have been disturbed downstairs, so I go upstairs. No—nothing missing that I notice on a casual inspection.

Then I remember that I didn't check the register. Funny that the cash is the last thing I think of. I trot back down the stairs—I love how these knees just bend as if it's the easiest thing in the world—and out to the shop. The old brass register opens with the sound of metal sliding against metal. The same small stack of bills I always leave for the next day's change is still there. If someone broke in, he wasn't much of a thief. A thief wouldn't have missed such an obvious payoff.

And what's this on the counter? Everyone has a message for me today, it seems. After reading it, I glance to the doorway. The extra set of keys that had gone missing has been returned through the mail slot just like the note says. I walk over and snatch them up, slipping the key ring around a finger so that I don't forget to hang them back in their proper place.

I look over the plastic name badge that was also left on the counter, but I don't recognize this man. And how tacky—really? Cassie has taken to plastic name tags? Ah well, it saves me the trouble of firing this Tom Collins, whoever he is. Since he had the keys, he isn't on the list of suspects, either.

It was probably just some local hooligan who was quickly scared off by the cops. Good. Hopefully he'll try again, and I'll have great fun putting him through his own personal Scared Straight program. There was precious little entertainment in this town when Eunice still exerted her influence. But she doesn't have any influence on me now. And it is— how would these humans say it—time to set the "inner goddess" free.

***

First things first. This box gets hidden. With the possibility of unknown persons pushing themselves into my business, I need to get that taken care of right away. Up to my room I go. I hold the Ab Khr in both hands and tread carefully up the stairs. It's only clay. It can be broken. And until the quickening ceremony, the heart cannot protect itself.

I place it on the bedside table while I make fast work of the vent cover. Then I step down onto the bed and drop the screwdriver on the pillow to grasp the Ab Khr and place it in its resting place. The two hearts are now side by side after all these years. The screws go back in quickly. My hiding place is secure.

Once that's taken care of, it's time to start putting less important things back together again as they were. If Cat had been standing watch over the house while I was gone, I'd know exactly who to punish. It's time he comes home.

He isn't near. I'd feel him. But how far could he have gone? Into the woods, probably, to feed himself on wild creatures until he feels his human side slipping away and needs my help preserving it. Then, he'll be home. His vain hope of being a man again always works in my favor. I suppose I could have left a window open for him before I left, but he deserved to be punished for running away. He'll be glad enough of shelter after spending so much time out in the elements.

Time to sort this out: at least I know where each of the items I'll need is kept after putting them all back in their proper places. I walk quickly through the shop, collecting ingredients. There's plenty of time before midnight to get in a small locating ritual and send out a beacon to force Tom home.

I clear the parlor table and sit on a velvet chair facing it. Oh my, this body loves its sensual pleasures. I never realized how comfortable this chair is.

On a lace mat, I place the brown candle on its golden holder. After lighting it, I sprinkle rosemary, jasmine, and other herbs into the flame by crunching the leaves into small bits between my thumb and forefinger. As the powdered herbs alight in the fire, sparks glow with the color of their magical essences. I stop sprinkling and wave the now-extinguishing orbs toward my face, where I breathe them in. Oh my—it's an exquisite sensation as the magic hits my bloodstream.

The slightly ochre tinge of the questing magic tints my vision. I close my eyes but the image of the room remains. Yellow sparks guide me like fireflies and my mind follows along its path, seeing each item as I pass it in the shadow land of the magic. The trail of light moves into the shop and passes under a shelf, briefly illuminating a dust bunny made primarily of Tom's fur. False positive. It will move on.

But it doesn't. The light extinguishes. The spell fades.

Tom is gone?

An involuntary gasp takes me. It can't be true.

All those years I kept him alive, putting up with his disobedience, and he's gone now that I need him?

No. No, he was just outside the shop a few days ago. The pigeon snagged a piece of him. He must have finally discovered a way to hide from me.

If he isn't dead, when I find him, he's really going to wish that he was.

***

The night air is warm. Such a shame we'll be wearing robes instead of prancing around in our skins. I'd dearly love to show off my new one, get the warlocks—and the witches who are inclined that way—worked up for no good reason. Sadly, even in the sixties, the Giles coven didn't indulge in the "free love" revolution during ritual. Too many married members, and the high priestess before me was an awful prude.

These east coast witches be damned. They've always been far too prim and proper. The French had an easier way about them. That's what attracted me to them in the first place. That and the little slip of a French girl finding my Ab Khr after it languished in a seaman's trunk in the attic for too many years. I enjoyed that skin and the skins of her female descendants for generations until I hitched a ride to the states with Eunice.

Tripping along lightly as I imagine Cassie might do in this situation, I approach Robert where he's standing with his SUV door open, donning his robe. On his left hand, he wears the ring that denotes his role of leadership. I don't have mine, but I'll get it back soon enough.

I wonder who's wearing it, although I really

shouldn't. I'm sure it will be Gillian. I forgot to check her fingers when she was in the shop. How fun to take it back from her. All the time she'll be thinking she's given it to someone nice who'll lead the coven in the right direction. I hold back a laugh. I dare say it might sound just a shade maniacal if I let it free here in the dark.

"Good evening, Robert. Where's that son of yours?"

"Too many other things to do. It's hard to keep the young people interested these days."

I can't imagine Kevin losing interest in taking his father's place when Daddy's gone. After all, he poisoned me for not moving swiftly enough to help him take it. I make a mental note to find out what Kevin's really up to. And then I'll decide how I can best use it to my advantage.

But for now, I play along. "You know that *I'm* happy to be here! I just wish Granny had told me about it a long time ago." I wonder if I got the gosh-gee-willikers tone right.

"Yes, I wish she had, too. You could have grown up in the choir instead of being on your own with your talents for so long." He ties his robe loosely around his waist and shuts the car door, offering me his arm in escort. Even in private, he was always a gentleman. I doubt age has changed him that much. Even if he hadn't been a gentleman in the sack, I'd still save this new body for Ba'al, as difficult as it's turning out to be. It responds to everything male.

But there shouldn't be much time left to wait. My husband and I will be like virgins again in our new bodies. I'll hold on to my fleshly explorations until then—or, at least until Tom returns. I take the arm I'm offered, and we walk toward the clearing, the other witches falling into a loose group around us.

It suddenly occurs to me that "Cassie" is the only younger person in attendance. Ah well, it's an elderly group these days. Kevin is younger by this coven's standards, but even he is in his late thirties.

Perhaps I can change that now that I have something soft and juicy to offer the potential warlocks in town. And, of course, eligible warlocks draw the young women. The possibilities are rather exciting. And when Ba'al returns in Tom's succulent flesh....

Oh my, I'm getting ahead of myself. I'm really not used to the chemicals running around in a young body anymore.

No one has their hood up yet. It's still meet and greet time. You'd think this was a gathering of the DAR complete with finger sandwiches.

Zelda and her daughter are either late or not coming. I spent a great deal of time grooming them over the years, pretending to take an interest in their lives. Perhaps they left the coven out of loyalty to me when I died? If they did, I can coax them back quickly. In fact, all of my devotees are missing tonight. But they'll return soon enough, when they see that I'm back in all my glory.

"Evening, Cassie," Natalie says as she saunters by. Wait a minute! Natalie's wearing my ring? Why would the coven put that buffoon in a position of power? It makes no sense. She's stolen something from everyone in the coven at some point. Kleptomania, my ass. The woman is just a thief. Although obviously, I'm not judging her. She's nowhere near the thief that I am: I've stolen an entire coven member, and no one has a clue.

I'd always thought Gillian would be everyone's choice for high priestess if Eunice stepped off before she did. It was her I was hoping to go up against to regain my power. Victory won't be anywhere near as sweet if I'm taking the power from Nat. There were times I even admired the old harpy.

Finally, Robert and Natalie draw their hoods up and others follow suit. Our priest and priestess walk among us, handing us each white candles, the color of cleansing and purification.

We form a ritual circle and Robert makes an inner circuit in the glow of his taper, lighting the candles we extend as he goes. I prefer a nice red candle myself. I have several waiting for Ba'al when he comes home.

The one who requested to be cleansed, Janice, walks to the center of the circle, seats herself cross-legged on the grass, and pulls her robe off her shoulders down to her waist, revealing sagging breasts and a stretch-marked belly. Her downward-facing nipples stiffen as the breeze blows across them.

I wish this was all over. Cleansings bore me. The chant begins, but I don't know the words to this one. Custom-made, probably, for Natalie to show off her bespoke casting skills.

Oh, let it be over. It's making me sleepy.

WHEN CASSIE—I still can't bring myself to think of her as Eunice—slumps to the ground, I creep cautiously out of the woods to join the circle. It will help to have as many people as possible who care about Cass lending their energies when Natalie attempts to cleanse her of Eunice's presence. Even someone with no magic. Love is a kind of magic in itself.

"Tom, get her and carry her to the center. Quickly. I don't know how long Eunice will sleep."

While I carry her to the middle of the ring as Natalie directed, Janice rejoins her peers, and the others start interspersing black candles with the white ones. Gillian told me earlier, when we were packing the items Natalie would need, that if what Eunice did to Cassie was a hex, the black candles would help. She just shrugged when I asked what affect it would have if it was something else.

Natalie claps her hands. "Everyone, join the circle now, very close. Take the hand of the person next to you and don't let go."

She begins the spell then, speaking quietly at first.

Outside the ring, the wind picks up, and Natalie's voice grows in strength to match it. Dead leaves swirl along the ground and the branches sway in the trees. Inside the ring, the candle flames stand straight, the trails of soot barely flickering as they head for the sky.

Cassie shudders and opens her eyes. I'm ready for this. My hood is pulled far down over my face, and I'll turn around and disappear quick if it's Eunice when she awakes. Everyone is prepared with the cover story: the group realized that Cassie's faint during the cleansing could be nothing less than a sign that she was still deeply burdened by the death of her grandmother. She needs a cleansing, too. The deep, black-candle kind.

She sits up and looks around, her eyes wide. "Omigod. You did it! Thank you, omigod…you have no idea what she is!"

I race to her without hesitation. I know it's Cassie. There's nothing of Eunice left in her voice or movements. I pull her head to my shoulder and glory in her arms pulling me close. I don't want to tell her this isn't permanent, that Eunice is just asleep. So, for precious seconds, I rock her in my arms, pretending for the both of us that this moment will never end, too overwhelmed to speak.

I feel a hand on my shoulder. Gillian. "Tom," she says softly. "Nat has to talk to her. We may not have much time."

I move to sit beside Cass, keeping her tight against me as Natalie comes forward. Cassie's eyes catch mine when I turn to brush my lips against her hair. "I know," she says. "I can feel her in here. She's not gone, right?"

I pull her closer in response. She sighs.

Natalie moves to question her. "The first thing you said was that we have no idea what she is. You're right. What is she?"

"Whatever she is, she's not my grandmother. She's the thing that was inside my grandmother. Something old, vile, and ugly. But definitely not human. I get flashes of her thoughts sometimes, even though I seem to be keeping her out of mine— it's all I can do against her, but at least she can't find out about any of you from me." She closes her eyes for a minute like she's in pain, then she continues.

"It's mixed up, and I don't always understand it, but she thinks of herself as a goddess. Maybe she is. But sometimes…there's no word for what she is. But if you could call any creature a devil…" She turns to Gilly abruptly. "Gilly, she has it in for you." She turns back to me. "And Tom, she's planning something even worse for you than what she's already done. You both need to get out of Giles."

I grasp her even tighter. "No. Hell no. I'm going to pull that bitch out of you if it kills me. There's no reason for me to keep going if you're gone." As I say it, I realize I've never before said anything so true. I spent forty-five years hanging on to the hope I'd escape Eunice, but now that I have, if I can't save Cassie too, I might as well be done. Why would I want my life back if I can't spend it with her?

She twists her fingers in my hair, and we lock eyes before we move in again for a kiss. Not the right place, not the right time, but more right than any other kiss could be. I linger there, not caring about our audience. Not caring about anything except her.

When we part, I want to speak, but my throat is constricted with emotion. I communicate with my eyes, and hers return the feeling, unwavering.

Then she whispers, "If you're going to help me, you need to hurry. Because the longer I stay in here, the smaller I feel. It's like she's trying to dissolve me."

"We'll figure this out. I swear it. Just hang on." I cradle her and smooth her hair, unable to stop smiling despite my fears. Cassie's here in my arms. Every moment is a miracle.

Suddenly, her eyes widen, and she trembles. "She's waking up. I can feel her. I'll fight to keep her down, but you have to go! I'm not strong like my granny was. I can't hold her back from hurting any of you." I resist her as she pushes me away. How can I let go of her knowing that this could be our last moment together? "Now, Tom! She's going to do something terrible to you with the box she brought back from Egypt. She's going to do what she did to me." Then she pushes me hard, her eyes pleading.

I need more time so I can tell her how I feel, but I don't hesitate any longer. If I get caught now, I'll never be able to help her. I'll never be able to show her that I love her. That doesn't make what I have to do any easier. I run for the woods, say my words, and shift. A small black cat runs out of a discarded robe and disappears into the bushes at the edge of the clearing.

***

I find a safe place in the shadows and listen in as Eunice wakes up. The wind sighs through the trees, but Cat has excellent hearing. I swivel an ear to tune in the sound from the witch's circle.

"What the hell? Get away from me!" Very un-Cassie like. Then she remembers herself. "I'm sorry. You all startled me, standing so close like that."

The well-faked and much-rehearsed concern begins.

"Are you all right, dear?"

"Anything injured in the fall? You gave us quite a start!"

"At least it happened where we can do a really effective healing ritual if you need one."

She brushes herself off and stands up. "No, I'm fine. Fine. You don't need to fuss over me. I'm just overwrought. I had a...breakup with my boyfriend, Dan. And, of course, there's Granny's sudden death. It's been upsetting."

Gilly steps in. "At least let me take you home now, sweetheart."

"No, I can drive." Even from a distance, I'm sure I hear the Cassie-thing gritting her teeth.

The gathering breaks up. People lower their hoods and split off into loose groups, walking toward the parking lot.

Natalie's really laying it on. I know she's enjoying herself. When it comes to keeping things hidden, Natalie is top shelf goods. "Janice, dear, we'll rearrange your cleansing. At the full moon?"

"Yes, Nat. Thanks. I'll see you then."

It's not the best outcome, but we didn't get caught, either. It's progress. And we know for sure now what's at stake—one amazing girl who's still alive in there. One caring girl who thinks of my safety before she thinks of her own. I don't deserve her. And I sure won't lose her.

Cat hears the rustle of night things and our adrenalin-heightened senses track them through the brush, begging Cat's body to follow.

Robert will be home before me tonight.

I'M COVERED IN THE gushing concern of the choir, and it feels disgusting. I need a shower. I drop my clothes on the floor in the parlor and travel upstairs to the bathroom naked, air rushing against all of my fresh, new parts. Cassie's certainly kept up with the latest trends in hair removal, and I'll continue the practice for a while, at least. It was the expected thing in my distant past as a nod to hygiene, but it's been several lifetimes since I've bothered. I feel like a Chihuahua.

We'll see how my lover likes it. Tom should be home any minute now. I know him. He won't go too long as Cat. Plus, he'll be concerned for me, I know he will. He tried to protect me against Kevin's venom, after all, when he discovered that Kevin was poisoning me. That wasn't a surprise. He'd always served me well and endured his reprimand when he strayed.

However, today's events confuse me. Why would I faint like that? Was it some backwash from the cleansing spell? Some undiagnosed physical complaint of Cassie's?

Oh blood of the gods, if she's pregnant...

Why should I be alarmed? How repulsively human of me. It's a small matter. I can easily rid myself of the thing. Tansy and pennyroyal are out: I don't want to accidentally poison her. I didn't groom her all those years to bury her right after taking her. No. Mugwort? Ashwagandha root? It depends on how far along she is. I'll sort it out if I need to. And, of course, there's always that newfangled medical abortion that's made the need for a visit to the witch woman obsolete.

I can't believe I have to make a trip to the drugstore at my age. I'm not going to wait until the thing starts to squirm.

It's time I found out what's happened since I've been gone.

***

It's a short trip down the street to the corner drugstore for the test. I imagine the girl would be anxious while waiting for the results, but I feel nothing. It's amusing, really, the way mortal women look forward to pushing another snot-nosed brat into the world.

When the time is up and there's no plus sign on my stick, I'm neither relieved nor saddened. But I'm glad that I won't be risking this body to get rid of the thing. I like the way it fits.

Now, it's time to procure the help of a sneaky little weasel who isn't smart enough to put anything over on me. Kevin will do nicely.

When he opens the door, he looks alarmed to see me. Or, more correctly, to see Cassie.

"Hello Kevin, I have a proposition for you."

His look changes from alarm to suspicion. "What kind of proposition?"

"I need you to fill me in on what's been happening in Giles. There may also be some small favors to perform. In exchange, I'll make sure you are soon ensconced as high priest, as I told you I would when we made our previous arrangement."

"I don't understand. What are you babbling on about? We're hardly on speaking terms. I've followed your rules. My father made sure of that. He won't let me break them any time soon."

"You don't recognize me, dear? I'm Eunice."

He narrows his eyes. "Eunice is dead."

"Was dead. Look closer."

"This is a trick. I'm not falling for it. Tom will pop out of the bushes any minute to pound the hell out of me for looking at you." He slams the door.

Curious.

Why would he mention Tom? Why would

Cassie tell Kevin, of all possible confidantes, about her werecat housemate? What has she been up to? And how did she discover any of this, anyway?

And I do want to get my nose into what's going on between Kevin and Robert. It intrigues me. I like a good intrigue. I like it even more when I can stir the pot. I do so love to see what's on the boil beneath the lid of any black kettle. It's often quite delicious.

It's clear that Kevin is going to be of little use to me until I sort him out, and I haven't the time nor patience for that just now. I suppose I could prove I'm Eunice easily, but why bother? He would probably just end up being a liability again. Zelda and that slattern daughter of hers can help me just as well.

Now, here's a thought: I was going to find a hobo or an orphan to provide a sacrifice during the quickening ritual. This feckless little man might be of use to me after all.

***

"No, I'm not dead! Not anymore!" I slam the phone down. A good slam is the one benefit of an old-fashioned corded phone. So satisfying to have on hand when everyone you speak to is an idiot.

I rush to collect a silk scarf for my trip. I rescued a few from the bottom of a drawer where I found some of Eunice's more valuable or memorable items of clothing—including the feather hats that Cat had so much difficulty staying away from. Suitably attired in a crisp suit with my hairstyle-preserving scarf tied just so and my makeup and powder impeccably applied, I head off down the sidewalk after locking the front door of the shop behind me.

When Zelda opens the door, she looks like she's seen a ghost. Now, that's more like it. I must be projecting an increased aura of the old me now.

"Let me in," I say, coldly. "Right this minute."

"Of course. I...I...do come in."

She steps aside, and I head for her shabby living room. I had no idea she lived this way. No wonder she was so hungry for any scrap I could give her. Her home screams ready-to-assemble.

At her insistence, I perch on the edge of her suspicious-smelling couch next to a big calico. I'm sure one of the outcomes of my visit will be flea bites, but I need to find out what happened when I was gone. I can't continue forward in the dark.

I feel myself glowering. I try to relax and present a more appealing appearance. "First things first—let me assure you that although I look like Cassie, and the rest of the town will know me as Cassie, I'm very much your old friend, Eunice. You know I am. I could see it in your eyes."

"I...you..." She gapes and hems and haws.

I lean in closer, conspiratorial now. "Do you remember when dear Dora came down with that nasty case of pregnancy just as her rich and celibate boyfriend was ready to propose?"

Her eyes widen. She's catching on.

"I did her such a nice service with my potion, didn't I?"

"Yes, you did."

"Go on then, say my name."

"Yes, you did," she says, then continues with emphasis, "Eunice. But how…"

"How have I ever done anything? With a strong will and a huge amount of power. Now, fetch me tea. Then call that useless daughter of yours and get her over here. We're going to talk."

An hour after the daughter arrives with her nails half-painted, I'm no wiser than I was before. Neither of them know anything about Tom or Kevin's relationship with Cassie. Neither of them know what Robert won't let Kevin do. They do report that certain members of the coven have been on the outs under the new leadership and have been subtly discouraged from attending. Maureen and Dora have felt unwelcome along with Zelda and her spawn, although Dora was never a special follower of mine. She didn't like Natalie much, though. But everyone else was certainly team Gillian, and I'm sure *they* were just waiting for me to pop off.

None of this makes sense. But at least I know where my followers stand. With a little prompting, they'll be back in the coven at the full moon to lend "Cassie" their support when she asks for it. I doubt that Natalie would actually block them from the circle. Subtle has no power against the direct approach.

What was that song about the moon Tom liked so much in the seventies? He would sometimes dance me around to it when he wasn't blaming me for his lot. I remember; I feel a bad moon a'risin'. My, oh my. Poor Natalie. That moon is rising soon.

MY BLACK FUR BLENDS in to the shadows in the narrow space between Eunice's big Victorian and the smaller one next door. Both of them are converted shops now—no one in Giles wants to live that close to each other. Too many secrets in this town. Who would want the neighbors listening in? Eunice is one of the few owners who still lives in the downtown area.

When she walks past the break between houses, I pull Cat in as small as he'll go and try to disappear into the patch of darkness around me. Cat alarms me with an impulse to dart out behind her and catch the hem of a pants leg as she passes, but I distract him with the thought of his blue bowl inside the house, imagining the fishy scent of his favorite glop. It's a good thing Cat's impulses can shift like leaves in the wind. He settles again, dinner on his mind.

I know Natalie promised that Eunice won't be able to sense me now, but I'm still not willing to take any chances. What Cassie told me about her has sharpened the edge of fear I've been living with since my caring girlfriend turned away from me that night in the attic and a devil turned back.

I look out from around the corner when enough time has passed, and Eunice is well down the street. At the corner, Robert greets her and they enter The Diner of Earthly Delights together. I've got my cell phone strapped to my collar so Robert can contact me.

I considered using the invisibility suit, but there's no way to test if it works on Eunice without potentially giving myself away. Better to assume that since she created it, she's also immune to its effects.

I can't believe I'm counting on Robert to make sure this thing goes off without a hitch. If she balks and heads home too soon, the only thing between me and slavery is his arthritic thumbs tapping me out a text in time to get me out of there before she arrives. Although he's been the soul of hospitality since I started staying at his house, and I know I owe him, I still can't fully trust him.

I'm swift as I run around the house and leap to the window Eunice usually leaves open for Cat. Cat is ecstatic. He's still thinking of dinner. He's going to be disappointed today. We leap into the parlor, and I head him toward the stairs instead of the kitchenette.

He cooperates until I get to the top of the stairs, but he decides he's focused long enough now and bats at the phone swinging around on his collar, hoping to take a break for some fun on the landing. Too bad for him it hangs in too close to our body, and he can't quite figure out how to reach it.

Whose idea was it to combine a tiny typewriter with a tiny phone and make people carry them around, anyway? The alarm function is useful, but I don't need to carry an alarm clock, or a phone, or a typewriter around all the time. If someone needs to talk to me and it's important enough, I'll respond to a message as soon as I can. And if it isn't important, why bother? I don't understand why everything has to happen the minute you think of it. Cassie says I'm too "old skool". I have no idea what that means.

Cassie. Always there in my thoughts. Cat's pulled me off the point again. I focus and say the shift words in my head: *good Tom*. After the transformation, I fumble with the stupid keyboard on the phone to send Robert a text, "I'm in."

He sends back, "crfl."

Sure. Whatever that means.

I glide up the stairs and into Eunice's old room. Cassie had redone it, but it's back in full Eunice mode now. The spare set of bedding has returned from its attic storage spot, bringing with it Eunice's satin and velvet debauchery. I freeze for a minute, terrified. She's preparing herself for me again. All the reds that Cat can't see are back in place. They were her special treat for me whenever she let me be a man.

Like hell. Not going to happen. I go to the closet and start sifting through what's stored there. I find nothing. I was sure this would be where she'd put the box now that she's back to nest in her lair. As important as it's turned out to be, she'd want to keep it close.

I look under the bed, but it's not there. The same with the other two bedrooms. Cassie's room is how she left it. Mine is still as empty as it was when I moved into hers.

I've got to go prowling through the rooms downstairs to try to find it. I don't want to. This house feels like a cage again instead of the home it had become.

My hand goes to my neck for the phone, just to reassure myself my early warning system is still in place.

My heart skips a beat.

It's not there.

But where? Where is it? I can't leave it in the house. I have to find it.

I rush back to Eunice's room, and there it is in the middle of the red and blue flowered, oriental carpet.

With a text.

From Robert.

Two words.

GET OUT.

The bell on the shop door jangles below as the door swings opens.

I turn off the phone and quickly affix it back to my collar. It better stay put this time.

I shift.

The only open window is downstairs. Why didn't I think of that before shifting? I'd have to run right in front of her to get to it. I don't have time to shift, open a window, then shift again to escape. And if I run across the landing to another room and she's already gotten to the stairs...

I'm trapped.

***

The closest place to hide is under Eunice's bed. Cat is hyped on my terror, the fur at the back of his neck standing at attention. I'm glad he's poised for a fight if something wicked this way comes. Anything can happen with Cat—he could be ready to snuggle up and purr instead of to fight. Thank the Goddess he goes along with me on this one. He doesn't always bend to me when he's in charge.

Cat stays put, listening, as Eunice prepares herself for bed, making evening ablutions, slipping one of Eunice's gowns on over Cassie's head. I watch her feet pull up from the floor as she finally eases herself into bed.

Any minute.

Any minute, I expect Cassie's head to appear suspended upside down, Eunice's smile on her face as she reaches under the bed to grab me, her preparations for sleep nothing but a sham.

Fortunately, Cat's heart is small. It doesn't thud loudly enough to get her attention.

The very thought of Eunice touching me with Cassie's stolen body makes me want to kill her. If I'd had the guts to fight her when it involved just me, I might have saved Cassie from all of this. But I was so determined to stay human and not give in to being the predator, the cat. Now, I wish I'd done it, treated her like Cat treats a mouse and gone at her when her guard was down. I'd take her out right now if I could do it without harming Cassie.

Instead, I'm stuck under the bed waiting for that monster to fall asleep. I keep Cat still and away from the warm body above by filling him with thoughts that the thing the human above most wants from him is for him to move around.

Obviously, being a cat, his only real choice is to do the opposite.

***

After an hour or so, when the Cassie-thing's breathing has settled into a regular rhythm, I know I have to take my shot. I wish it was darker in here, but Eunice had the habit of keeping some light on in case she woke up hungry. Not so she could get down the stairs. So she could get to me. That kind of hunger.

I've never been as grateful for Cat's stealth abilities as I am right now. His cat's paws make no sound as I slip out from under the bed and make my way toward the door, my body low to the carpet, ready to spring and burst into a run if there's any sound behind me.

But there is no sound. Only Cat's heart racing to my fear. And tonight, fear doesn't cripple me. I travel swiftly down the stairs, out the downstairs window, and chase the darkness through the backyards of Giles as I head back to my temporary home with Robert.

***

The open window at Robert's place never looked so welcoming. I leap through and shift, get dressed, and head for the kitchen.

"Oh my Goddess. Tom!" Gillian leaps from a chair and charges toward me, arms outstretched to capture me in a hug.

Robert turns, too, and a small smile moves across his face. "Good to see you." He extends a hand for me to shake, and I take it once I extricate myself from Gilly's grasp.

I haven't been part of any kind of community

for so long, it never occurred to me that anyone would worry about me. I probably shouldn't have stopped to let Cat hunt. And why are Gillian and Robert suddenly so cozy?

Gillian throws up her hands when I don't offer any information. "Well—where have you been? We were gutted. When Robert told me where you were and that you didn't meet him when Eunice went back to the house...." She stops then, halfway through pouring hot water into a tea cup, and looks up at me with a stern look. "You didn't just head to the woods for a hunt and leave Robert like that to worry, did you?"

I'm afraid to tell her that I did some of that. She doesn't need to know. But I've learned an important lesson if there's ever a next time. That's right, just like a kid—call if you're going to be late.

I give her mostly truth. "The phone fell off my collar, and I didn't know it was gone until it was too late. I had to hide under the bed until I was sure Eunice was asleep."

She's apologetic then. "Oh, Tom, I'm sorry. You must have been terrified." She sets a steaming cup of water in front of me with an herb-stuffed infuser sitting on top, filling the kitchen with the scent of roses. "That will calm your nerves if they need it."

Robert sits across from me and Gilly runs off to the kitchen to boil more water for the both of them. "She worries about you. You're still very important to her."

"I know. But not in the same way I was when she was young."

"No," he agrees. "Not in that way."

Why does he look relieved?

THE SHOP BELL RINGS to the first customer of the day, and in she comes, Gillian.

"Hello, sweetie! Are you feeling all better after the fainting spell on Thursday?"

"Fine. Yes." I really must find a way to discourage her from coming around every five minutes.

She pokes her head behind the shelves, then stoops to look underneath them. Her gigantic derriere confronts me when she does. Her mouthy end asks, "Still no Cat? Or is he just hiding today?" It's like she's taunting me. She pulls out the bag of treats she'd brought with her last time and unseals it. "The smell of these should bring him running if that's the case."

"Still hasn't returned, I'm afraid. Please let me

know if you spot him around town."

"Of course, pet. I hope nothing's happened to him."

"Cat's tough. Granny Eunice used to say that Cat had nine lives and every single Cat since the sixties was the very same one! Imagine that. And Granny loved her Cat so. She used to say that having him around was better than having a boyfriend because all he needed was a little catnip, and he'd be eating out of her hand." I smirk as I enjoy my own private joke.

"Is that so? Yes, I suppose Eunice did say a lot of things that made no sense. I'm sure that I'd rather have a boyfriend who loves me than a cat who sees me as a source of food and shelter. Not that there are many men my age still around. But even so...." She gives what I'm sure she thinks is a winning smile. It's repugnant.

I turn away so she doesn't see my face as I start to steam. "I really need to prepare a few of the perishables today. You don't mind if I step into the back room, do you?"

"Not at all, sweetheart," she says, "In fact, I just stopped in to make sure you're all right, and I've accomplished that. You look very well. See you on the full moon! I do hope Cat comes back soon."

I'm more than glad to be rid of her. It's as if she came in here just to rub my nose in it that my Tomcat hasn't returned yet. If she knew all of the details, well...the conversation would have been much more satisfactory. But I can't play my hand and ruin the chance for Cassie in this town just yet. The coven flicks its eyes away from a lot of what goes on—many of the members, even the ones who didn't follow me, had a darker spell or two they employed for their own benefit. Who wouldn't when all that temptation is constantly there, begging for attention?

Except, of course, for Gillian. That one was always so clean. When her husband was dying, she purchased some questionable items in the shop, but she returned them unopened. Yes, much too clean.

Still, the coven wouldn't look the other way at body snatching. Not that there's anything they could do about it, but being discovered would ruin my fun. I'd have to scorch this town and learn all the secrets of another one. That kind of thing takes years.

No, I'm not done with Giles yet. And there are still a few residents I'd love to see squirm. I'll have no trouble pulling that off now. The girl is quiet as a mouse in here. She doesn't have her grandmother's spunk. Eunice fought and was able rein me in far too often.

Once I've deposed Natalie, I'll move Gillian to the top of the list. I don't know what would destroy her world the way it did when I took Tom, but I'm sure I'll come up with an encore that is equally delectable. I admit that I enjoy devising clever ways for my victims to hoist themselves on their own petty human petards. It's all in figuring out what they've already got rigged to blow. Eunice pulled me off of my entertainments too many times, but there's nothing stopping me from having my fun now.

***

I'm beginning to hate the shop. Everyone is so nicey-nicey to Cassie. I think it's time to shutter it for a while or, at least, pay some teenage wage slave to work the counter while I play the lady of leisure. I have plans to make.

During my lunch hour, I add a pinch of a very special ingredient to the jasmine tea before I seal the bags. Giles is about to have a small outbreak of sweating sickness only slightly less virulent than the sweat of Tudor times: I can still squeeze enough fun out of Giles that I don't want to decimate the population. No, I'll do the Picardy sweat this time. The local hospitals will never have seen it, but with the improved health-care system of modern times, its victim should recover after an unpleasant day or two. I don't need to do anyone in just yet.

The Tudors needed something stronger for me to get what I wanted: it cleared the way to put Henry in power—that delicate Arthur never would have pleased me—and I wholeheartedly approve of how Henry handled his wives with only a little urging. Except for the ugly German. I was out of town during that fiasco.

I took pleasure in being behind the man with the power because the witch's body I took didn't contain enough magic for me to rule on my own. It was nearly as much fun being the hidden power behind the throne. I let go of another weak vessel when I felt the strength of the magic within Eunice. She'd joined with the coven where I'd jumped from mother to daughter across the generations since the end of the Tudor reign. Giles was my own little empire because of Eunice's powerful essence, and it will be again unless Ba'al wishes to move on. With the owner of my last body no longer holding me back, and the same abundant reservoir of magic in this new body, I can finally cut loose.

The shop bell rings. "Coo-ee, Cass. I'm here for my Magical Masque." Natalie's right on time for her weekly facial treatment. She's entirely dependent on me because of her vanity. If I refused her, her face would shrivel to a mass of wrinkles within a month. And, of course, someday, when she's most vulnerable, I will most certainly refuse.

"I've got it right here for you, Nat."

I package the beribboned jar in a small brown bag and hand it to her. She's asked for my secret many times, but I'll never share. As I hand it to her, I say, "Did you see the jasmine tea is on sale today? Can't beat the price. You should indulge yourself."

I push the tray full of artistically arranged gift bags toward her. I just need to let her see the price.

She loves a bargain almost as much as she loves a steal.

There. She bites. She picks up a package, looks at the sticker, and with the barest widening of her eyes, says, "Yes, go ahead, ring me up the tea, then. You know I like a deal."

"That will be thirty-two fifty-seven total."

"Here it is, dear." She counts out the money a coin at a time. The town klepto always knows to the penny how much money she has in that flashy red purse she's been hauling around since the sixties. "See you on the full moon, dear."

"Yes, for sure. See you then." I giggle a little for authenticity. It nearly gags me.

When she's gone, I throw the rest of the tea in the trash. I've already hooked the big fish I was angling for.

THE DOORBELL RINGS. Then rings again. And again. And then, whoever it is just leaves their finger on the bell and it keeps up one long rrrrrrrrrinnnnnnnnnnnngggggggggg. Robert gives me a what-the-hell look as he passes the doorway of the den where Gillian and I have been sitting companionably while we each take another whack at Robert's magic books. Being near her now helps me stay calm even though Cassie is in so much danger. She exudes an it-will-all-be-okay vibe that I want to believe.

Robert returns with Natalie in tow. She has a bag from Cat's Magical Shoppe in her hand and an intense look on her face.

"More bad news, I'm afraid," she says as she enters the room. She holds the bag out to Gillian.

"In that bag is a packet of jasmine tea that I believe was meant to start an infectious disease emergency in town. Or at least in me. I've sent Janice to buy up the rest of it, and I'm pretty sure that I'll find the same minuscule critters in there that I did in mine." Natalie harrumphs. "And I thought I just had to watch the face cream. I'm glad I'm such a mistrusting soul."

"Critters?" I ask.

"A virus. One I haven't seen before. I'm not sure it even exists in modern times. It may not even be naturally occurring, and if it is, it's been magically engineered to survive being boiled for tea. Either way, it knows how to party when it hits the blood supply. I hooked it up with a few drops under my old microscope, and it really discoed down. I'm meeting Janice out at her farm to quarantine and infect a pig. I'm hoping it will give me some idea of what it's meant to do to us.

***

The next morning, Gillian is at the breakfast table, her eyes following her finger down the center of a page of text. The smell of good coffee fills the air.

She looks up and says, "I didn't think Robert would mind if I let myself in and got started early. Couldn't sleep. You?"

"You have a key?" Now I'm really wondering

what's going on.

She holds up her index finger and thumb absently while she keeps reading and blue sparks jump between.

"Gotcha. No key needed. And who needs sleep?" Coffee. That's all *I* need. I grab a mug and start pouring.

Gilly's cell rings. After a hello, she tells the caller to hang on for a minute. "Go get Robert." she says. "Natalie's got news.

It's been impossible just waiting, researching, hoping for something that will help us understand what's going on so that we can do something for Cassie. If it's such big news we all need to be present, maybe this is it.

When I get back with Robert in tow, Gillian is just saying goodbye. "Nat's figured out what she needs to know from the pigs. She's going to give herself a dose of the tea. Apparently, this is aimed just at her. When Janice went back to buy the rest no more than an hour later, Eunice told her it was all gone, but Janice saw it right there in the trash behind the counter."

"Wait a minute. She's going to make herself sick? Can't she just fake the symptoms, too?"

"No. She thinks we need to go big on this, and she's willing to do it. If…" Gillian stops and makes quotation marks with her fingers "…'Cassie' looks closely at the effects of her handiwork—and you know how Eunice has to make sure everything is in its place—it needs to look realistic. She thinks the small dose will let it pass through her system quickly. And she intends to get to the hospital fast once it hits."

"Man," I say, shaking my head, having a hard time believing what these people will do to help Cassie, to help me. "Natalie's really falling on her sword."

Robert nods. "Maybe. I think it's more a joust with what's inside Cassie than an act of altruism."

Robert might be right, but I prefer to interpret her sacrifice as noble. Either way, she's doing more to figure out how to beat Eunice at her own game than anyone else. I set down my coffee and say, "Given the timing and that this was directed at Nat, Eunice may want her out of the way during tomorrow's full moon. If she's got something planned that our high priestess could interfere with, don't we need to make sure it backfires on her?"

"What could she be planning?" Gillian asks.

"No idea. But if she wants Nat out of commission on the full moon, it has to be something she needs the coven for. Maybe she'll try to con you all into letting her take Natalie's place in the ritual. That sure sounds like something Eunice would try to pull off."

Robert nods, stroking his unshaven chin. The heavy white stubble makes a scritching sound that makes my cat side restless. "It makes sense. She couldn't take the power position without Natalie gone. And if she talks her way into that, she could certainly talk her way into having them perform any ritual she has planned. We'd have a hard time stopping it without blowing our cover."

"Good. Let's put our heads together and make sure the coven isn't right there for the taking."

It wasn't any colder in this old house before I had it retrofitted for a furnace in the sixties while I transformed it from a family home to host the Magical Shoppe. I had to lose the second fireplace to run ductwork to the ceiling on the second floor and then back down for ceiling vents. But you can't hide much of anything in a radiator, and I have things I need to hide. Throughout the house, there are false vents that give no heat but make convenient holding places for special items. Cassie may have cleared the house of Eunice's things, but she didn't clear it of mine.

I set the first box on the bedside table, and then I step back up on the headboard to reach into the vent and carefully slide out its mate. *There you are sweetheart. Come to mama.* I can't stop myself checking on him now that he's so near.

I open the box and my beloved Ba'al's heart is bared to me—still surprisingly well preserved despite the thousands of years that have passed since we ruled together as Ba'al and Anat. It was my first name, sometimes nearly forgotten through the years as I've thrust myself first into one body, then another, each of them marking me with a name and a set of experiences. All of those human lives almost obscured that once, I was a goddess.

Sadly, even a God or Goddess can be incapacitated by the right wounds. I was incapacitated by death myself when Ba'al died, waiting to be discovered so that I could jump into a new body. Fortunately, after a time, tomb robbers found me.

I didn't like taking a male body. I discarded it as soon as possible. It didn't survive. Must have been the mummy's curse.

Fortunately, I had been able to keep my Ab Khr safe from the thief's companions. It allowed me to jump again quickly into something more suitable.

When I get my lover's heart beating again during the quickening, I'll help him move to his new home in Tom's handsome shell soon after. Will he find me too tame now? I'm in bed by ten after taking my nightly bath in lavender-scented bubbles instead of the blood of my victims. But oh, when we were young! There wasn't a god or a demon who could challenge us.

I take inventory of my factory-showroom fresh body. It's outrageous, a goddess reduced to inhabiting fragile humans to experience life. Sometimes I wish Ba'al had died with me so that we could have lain together in our tombs. If he'd accompanied me on that journey, maybe I could have been happy to release my essence to the universe.

Then again, who knows if I'd have wanted to follow him when the time came. It would be fickle of me, but I've certainly had my share of excitement without him.

Still, it's not like the good old days. There was a time when temples bore my name and thousands came to worship. Now, humans barely believe in gods.

Being worshiped was a hoot. Being mummified, not so much. At least my handmaiden got it right and put my heart into the Ab Khr before they sealed me into that tomb. I don't know why she stopped there and didn't say the words I'd prepared for her. I was sure she'd do exactly as I told her. Irritatingly enough, once I was dead, there was nothing I could do to make her follow through.

Two hundred years of darkness—also, not much fun. When I finally did alight back in the world, I definitely wasn't in my carefully chosen, comely body.

I close the box and lightly rest my hands on top, tracing the symbols. Life, Death, Rebirth. So simple. The secret of my people since the beginning of time.

That secret will bring my lover back to me once I've finished my preparations and can finally place him into the vessel I prepared for him so long ago. The two of us are going to paint this town red before we're through.

I put both of the boxes back in the vent and secure the vent cover across the front. Our hearts remain together as they should always have been.

There, everything I cherish is now safely tucked away until I can obtain what I need from the town choir. How they'll sing to my tune once I get my claws into them again! Here's hoping Natalie obliged me by sampling her tasty, terrible tea. That will make everything go much smoother.

***

I park the girl's car and step out into the gravel parking lot just after the sun sinks under the tree line. Some of the coven members have already gathered near the picnic tables. I walk toward them, and just as my eyes pick her from the crowd, Natalie sinks to the ground, breathing heavily. And she's sweating like the proverbial pig.

I hurry toward her exactly like that dull Cassie would have done. I hope I'm wearing the right expression of concern, but I'm not sure I'm getting the emotion right. They're such pesky things, emotions.

"What happened? Is she okay?"

Gillian has the sad old thing's head cradled in her lap by the time I get there. Robert has a hand on her forehead. "You're burning up!" he says. "It must be that bug that's going around. We'll get you to the hospital. Better safe than sorry. Can you walk?"

"I think so." Natalie stands, but she's shaky, and Robert puts an arm around her to stabilize her. Gillian props up the other side.

Natalie looks like she's melting. How fun. "It's so hot in this robe."

Gillian turns to me. "Don't worry about Natalie, sweetheart," she says, "I'm sure she'll be just fine. The good thing is, there's always another full moon."

I perform a supportive murmur, but it will be a cold day in Tuat when I give Natalie's safety a moment's attention. The three of them lumber off toward the parking lot. All three of them out of the way? Even better than I'd hoped. The rest of the coven are sheeple, who can only stand and baa without them.

Then, the other members of the coven begin to follow their leaders. No, that's not in their cards tonight. Time for me to intervene.

"No wait—we can't just forget about it. I've been so looking forward to being with you all here. Can't we observe the full moon without the leaders?"

Lydia says, "No priest, no priestess. That puts a kibosh on the ritual, don't you think?"

But Zelda steps in to follow my lead, just as I'd prepared her to do. Her eyes dart to me and then away as she speaks. "Why can't we? We did it before, remember? Right after Eunice died. Robert was out of town. And Darrin's here. He can provide the male force."

"No, I'm taking off. I wouldn't feel right without at least one of the designated priests or priestesses," Darrin says.

There's some shuffling of feet and then a few more voices agree, and the old rooster leads a short line of hens toward the parking lot. But there's still enough of them for my purpose.

"Well, now what? We're all women here with Darrin leaving. The ritual will be unbalanced."

I say, "Someone call Kevin. He's usually here, isn't he?"

Lydia volunteers, "No one really knows why Kevin stopped coming. It was kind of a surprise."

"Then it's a perfect opportunity to ask him to come back. I'm sure if you ask him to take his father's place, he'd come. Make sure you say it exactly that way." I give that last statement a little magical help, an extra push. It registers on her face as a sudden relaxation of all the small muscles. Her lids droop and her mouth gapes.

"I could call him," she agrees. Not that she had a choice. "I left my cell in the car, but I'll go get it.

You're right that he'd want to help out." She lifts the hem of her robe above her knees and heads toward the parking lot, saying, "Back in a minute."

That dowdy Maureen gives me unexpected help with the rest of them by reminding them she was hoping for a fertility blessing for her granddaughter. She waves around a stuffed bear she brought to have blessed so that she can later slip it under her daughter's bed. She gets a little choked up when she talks about how long she's waited for grandchildren.

Some of the others get on the horn to call the rest of the missing coven members.

It's a nice touch. I wish I'd planned it. Manipulating these stooges is just too easy.

***

When Kevin arrives, as I knew he would when the right carrot was dangled in front of him, I move close and say "Didn't I tell you I'd help you replace your father?"

He nods. His eyes continue to broadcast mistrust, but the greed for power glints there, too. He takes his place in the circle next to me. "Just don't expect me to handle any of the coven's sacred objects. I still can't touch anything invested with magic. And I can't join hands in the circle if magic is being passed through it."

My. Interesting. What had Robert done?

When the other absent witches arrive and all are

gathered, "Cassie" speaks in the formal language reserved for ritual. "I have a request for you on this most powerful of nights, brother and sisters of my circle. When Maureen's casting is complete, will you assist me with a blessing? Will you lend me your power?"

All of them assent.

Maureen moves to the center of the circle and places the teddy bear on the ground. "This will lie beneath my granddaughter's bed to bring a child to her. I ask your blessing, goddess."

"We ask your blessing, goddess," the other witches repeat in unison.

Maureen and Kevin read the blessing together from the paper Maureen provided. As they chant, the wind in the trees blows stronger. Under Cassie's hood, I smirk. This foolish woman has no idea the force she's called on. As Anat, I was known for granting increased fertility to the unhealthy and short-lived women of her time. Imagine what my blessing might do to a healthy twenty-first century woman with plentiful eggs? Such fun.

The bear shakes and jumps in place in the center of the circle as the chant ends.

None of the coven has seen that happen before. No one mentions it, but one or two pairs of eyes dart around the circle seeking reassurance. This fertility ritual is new to them. When most of them were young enough for childbearing, they were bent on avoiding pregnancy, not precipitating it.

Kevin signals the end of the ritual. "So shall it be."

After the others echo him, I begin. "I ask your power to draw down the goddess on this, the full moon. Will you lend me your power?"

They murmur their yeses.

I move my feet apart to shoulder length and lift my arms toward the moon. "I am the vessel. You are the goddess. I draw you down to inhabit me. Fill me with your beauty and your strength, your wisdom and honor, your humility and courage."

I initiate a shimmering mist around my borrowed body. It's filmy and vague, but it should be visible to the others in the circle. Also not a typical event for them. Their Goddess's ways are usually much more subtle.

"Goddess of the desert, goddess Anat, return from the moon and enter your servant. Allow me your gracious presence, O Great Goddess!" I'm hamming it up now, playing to the cheap seats. I know the increasing blue glow around Cassie's body will keep their attention.

I send the mist swirling and thrusting upward, reaching for the moon. I hear someone gasp as feelers of light grasp for the full, round orb as if it could be captured and kept. Then, abruptly, the light ceases. I pierce the darkness dramatically by projecting a reddish light from this vessel's eyes. I change her hair from brown to midnight black in the glow that now lights her. Simple enough magic for a goddess.

Every single witch in the circle takes an involuntary step back.

Time to announce my presence.

"I am the goddess Anat, drawn down to this girl as she beseeched." I like the ring of that—beseech. A good word no one uses anymore. "I would stay with you and know your coven. Are you worthy of the presence of a goddess?"

No one moves.

I look from person to person within the circle, maintaining the hypnotic red glow. As my eyes pass over them, compelling them, each kneels to me and makes a gesture of submission.

"We are not worthy, goddess. Teach us to be worthy," they chorus.

Really, it's just too easy.

Of course, I owe some of it to the moon's pull and the force of the witches in the circle, but no one needs to know that I need them to magnify my power. This body is strong in magic, but it doesn't contain the power of a goddess.

At my left hand, Kevin kneels and kisses the hem of my robe. I haven't even enchanted him yet. It appears I won't need to. He's always been a servile little runt—even when he was trying to kill me. I need his willing participation anyway. The magic is stronger when the sacrifice is made by choice.

"I'll do anything you say. I've been waiting all my life for someone with your power to lead me."

Isn't that just like the sniveling little worm? Show him a little power, and he wants to be the first in line to share. I place my hand on the top of his slick, bald head. "I knew you'd see sense. Now, tell me what your father did to make it impossible for you to touch magic?"

"I don't know what he did. He put his hand on my back and it tingled a little, but ever since then, I can't touch anything invested with it. It burns like hell. I have to let go right away or I end up blistered."

"A simple enough thing to undo. Turn around."

I place my hand at the small of his back and intone a few words, pulling the magical allergy Robert gave his son out of the seat of his magic. The red glow of the magic dissipates when it meets the air.

"There. I've fixed you. Test it for yourself. Go to Cassie's car and bring me the box hidden under the driver's seat. Quickly!"

Kevin scampers off. The rest of the witches continue to kneel, their eyes to the ground, still trapped in my thrall.

When Kevin returns, I tell him, "Go to the center of the circle and place the box before you. Then kneel and await my bidding."

Kevin does as he's told, silently. Such a ridiculous man. But he has a life essence to offer up, and that is all I need from him.

I raise my hands to the skies again and begin the

chant. As I do, the witches learn it and pick it up so that the light buzzes between and around them.

Kevin doesn't understand the words the circle chants. They're orderly, but they're nonsense to him. Unlike any language he has ever heard spoken. I intone them with great seriousness. If he understood them, he'd run.

By the time he realizes his mistake, it will be far too late.

***

The chant takes on a life of its own; I no longer need to lead it. I move into the circle where Kevin sits cross-legged, his eyes on the Ab Khr. I crouch behind him, my hands on his shoulders. I bend my mouth to his ear and whisper to him softly.

"You see? I told you that, in time, I would give you all the things I promised. Your father's place in the coven, a place in my more indelicate business, and this..." I brush the girl's firm breasts against his back and he leans into them. "It's really too bad you couldn't wait for it." I move my right hand from his shoulder and grasp the ancient pesheskef blade that I shoved into the pocket of my robe before leaving the house. Kevin startles when he feels the cold iron against his neck.

I press my mouth close to his ear again. "Did you think I didn't know about the poison? That I didn't know every time something extra went into

Eunice's tea?" I laugh. He winces at the close, explosive sound.

"Look, Cassie…Eunice…"

"Do you really think I'm some ridiculous human? That you could kill me? I allowed it because it served my purpose. I was tired of that shell, and my new one was ready for me."

"So, you'll show mercy? I was only following in your footsteps, doing what you would do."

I hate it when he whines.

"Of course, my lamb. You've always been my favorite."

He starts to answer, but he chokes on his blood instead as I slice through his throat. I lean in close and whisper, "How's that for mercy?"

Burble, burble, burble. The sound of my revenge. I watch the golden sparks build slowly at first, flitting like fireflies from Kevin to the Ab Krh, the box that contains my beloved's heart.

He presses his hands to his neck, attempting to stanch the flow. It does him no good as the blood pulses out between his fingers. His essence becomes the golden light of magic and streams toward the box to quicken Ba'al's silent heart and draw him home.

ROBERT HELPS NATALIE into his outsized SUV. Once she's in, Gillian slips in beside her, propping her up.

I'm under the front bench seat, peering out with my nifty I-see-just-fine-in-the-dark-because-I'm-a-cat eyes. Natalie has pulled her robe up to her knees, and her bare legs glisten with sweat just in front of me.

Robert steps along quickly to the driver's side, and Gillian starts talking, still tending to Natalie as Robert backs up, just a little too fast, the tires spraying gravel as he goes.

"Something went wrong. Eunice was trying to convince them to stay as we left. We were stupid not to let everyone in on the plan! Half the coven doesn't even know that's Eunice. Plus, Zelda and her daughter, who we know were loyal to Eunice,

135

showed up. And yes, I know it's the full moon and we always meet on the full moon, but they didn't show at the last one when we didn't invite them." She's addressing me, I know, but cats aren't known for their conversational skills. It's not like I can answer back.

I go to the window at the side of the van and risk a peek outside, claws dug in to the upholstery. We're well away now. Eunice won't catch me if I shift. I slink into the back and make myself human, then presentable in a t-shirt and jeans, and shuffle back to the front seat, hunched over under the low ceiling.

"You know her better than we do," Robert says, his eyes darting a glance to the rear view mirror to meet mine, "What do you think she's up to?"

"My best guess is she needs the coven's power for something she wants to cast."

Gilly turns to Robert, "That's alarming. We need to go back. We have to keep an eye on her."

I say, "Drive to the lot near the rental cabins. There's a path through the woods back to the clearing from there. It's the shortest way back that will let us avoid being spotted."

"We need to get Natalie taken care of first," Gillian says.

She's right. "Robert, pull over. We need to stop Darrin. Gilly, call him and tell him to pull over when he sees us at the side of the road."

She takes out her cell and makes the call. The

conversation is brief. "He's right behind us."

Robert pulls his SUV as far off the narrow road as he can get it. Natalie's doing worse now. When Darrin pulls his sedan up behind us, I help her to the waiting back seat. He hands her a bottle of water and says, "Don't worry. I've got this." Nat smirks despite the beads of sweat running off her face. Then they're gone.

Robert pulls a u-ie and heads back toward the road to the campgrounds that we just passed.

***

Gillian and Robert huddle together in the brush. They've taken the best viewing spot for themselves. It's dense enough to provide cover but with enough space to stand comfortably without pine needles and pricker bushes stabbing at every move. I whisper from behind, "Well, what are they doing?"

"Shush," Gillian says. She motions me closer to look through a break in the branches. Her brow furls and she squints toward the ritual space. "We made a foolish assumption about the need for a high priest and priestess. She's convinced them to stay and honor the full moon without us."

Looking out to the clearing, I watch with them as Kevin walks in from the direction of the parking lot with a box in his hands. I turn and whisper to Gillian, "That's just like the box I saw before Eunice took Cassie over. Could be the same one." She pats my arm to indicate she heard, her eyes never leaving the event unfolding in front of us.

Robert moves in closer to Gillian so that he can see, too, and she gives him a coy smile as he presses close to her, sharing her hiding place. He flicks a quick smile back. Why is Robert suddenly hot stuff?

The wind rises, chasing the branches of the trees, and I stop worrying about what's going on between the other two when the space the witches inhabit begins to swirl with light. Fireflies? No. Magic.

And then, too weird—it's as though a dome comes down around the circle and it's suddenly like looking through frosted glass. The witches are still there, lit by the awful light, but the distance and the veil around the ritual space make it impossible to tell what's going on. Then, at the center, one of the indistinct figures begins to glow.

Robert starts to move forward, but I stop him with a firm hand on the shoulder. "No, I'll go. I'll see what's happening. It won't help anything for her to figure out you've been working against her. It's dark outside whatever that dome is. Cat will be able to hide in the shadows."

I crouch to the ground and think *bad tom*, then shift, gritting my human teeth against the pain until they're replaced by cat's sharp, white ones.

I spring out of the brush on four legs, moving swiftly but close to the ground, my tail held out low to drift above the grass as I stalk.

Eunice is looking the other way when I approach the veil. It's not quite glass, but it's not quite air, either. I press a paw to it and try to push through. It gives, but I can't pierce it. Whatever Eunice is doing in there, none of us will be able to interfere.

From where I crouch hidden by a tall clump of grass behind the Cassie-thing's back, the fireflies of light swirl into longer plumes of flame, moving from the black-robed figure in the center of the circle to the box and disappear into its surface. The figure, I think it's Kevin based only on where he knelt in the center of the circle before the veil came down, pitches forward, hands to his throat, then falls to the ground, sparks leaping from his body until he stops moving completely.

When it's done, the golden light fades and the veil lifts. The witches look around at each other, then at Kevin. One of them starts to wail, one of them bolts toward the parking lot, but the Cassie-thing screams out, "Stop."

The witches freeze. Then, they move to her one by one, kneel, kiss the hem of her robe, and walk unhurried to the parking lot.

Once they've all knelt to her, the Cassie-thing turns her head on a sweep around the site. Oh Goddess, her eyes. I shrink as deep into the shadow of the lump of grass I lurk behind as I can. When those lit-up red orbs swing my way, I can only hope she doesn't catch a glimpse of me. They don't pause as they sweep over my patch of ground. She blinks them and the red light is gone, her hair suddenly appearing lighter than before. She looks deceptively like my Cassie again as she walks quickly to her car with the box clasped firmly in her hands.

***

Once Cassie's car leaves the parking lot, I dash toward the misshapen mass where Kevin had knelt. The thing I find there isn't Kevin anymore. His skin is like parchment, dried out and stretched tight across his bones. From his appearance, you'd think he'd been dead for years. He looks like the pictures of the unwrapped mummies from Eunice's archeology books.

I hear someone coming up behind me and look over my shoulder. It's Robert with Gillian trailing. He doesn't need to see this. But Cat is too small to stop him or hold him. I shift, but by the time I'm in control again, it's too late to get in his way and try to soften the blow.

He stumbles over an uneven patch in the grass and catches himself ungracefully before he falls to his knees next to his son, head in his hands, his sobs the only sound now that the wind has blown itself out.

Cat's predatory instinct has given me a high tolerance for all the stages of death, but it hasn't given me any understanding of grief. I have no idea what I'm supposed to say to comfort him. Not that anything I could say in the nude would be a good idea anyway. And I'm definitely not going in for a hug.

Gillian kneels next to Robert and puts a hand on his back. He turns to her and buries his head in her shoulder. She places her arms around him, rocking him the way she would a child. I turn to the woods and leave them alone as I go to gather my clothes.

***

It's unusual for a small town like Giles to have its own coroner, but the members of the choir are happy to pay the extra tax for his salary to assure that magic gone wrong doesn't become magic exposed. Not that the coveners are prone to murder, but a few miscalculations and...well, mistakes get made.

Like many of the residents of our fair town, Dr. Don knows just enough about the goings on around him to know that some things are better off not being written down. Even the non-magical residents have no interest in being scrutinized by the media. They're happy to let Salem ham it up for the business.

He stands up, shaking his head, and pushes his black-rimmed glasses up his nose as he walks to where Robert sits on a fallen log outside the ring that witches' feet have worn into the grass. Gillian still hovers over him. I think she probably won't leave him alone until she sees him safely home.

I step in front before he reaches them and guide him to the side, out of earshot. "Let's give him some time before he has to deal with all of this."

He shoves his glasses up his nose. "I'm calling this one. No ambulance needed. Another obvious case of drowning. That lake is becoming a real hazard."

"Thanks, Doc."

He inclines his head in Robert's direction. "I'd like extend my condolences before I go. He's a friend, you know."

I nod, but when the two men shake hands, Robert's grip is so visibly limp that you might think he'd been deboned.

The doc tells him, "I'll get him covered and contact the rescue squad. I can keep him at the morgue until you've had time to make arrangements."

Robert shakes his head. "No. I have an expert who needs to take a look."

The coroner squeezes Robert's hand again, and then I hustle him away and walk him back to the parking lot. It's easy to get turned around in the woods at night, but I know every inch. I've stalked all of them many times over the past forty-five years. Before we're out of sight, Gillian comes running after me, holding her keys out.

"There's a blanket in the back of my car. Please bring it back with you. Oh, and there's some of those tie-thingies with the hooks on the end. You know, the rubber-bandy things."

Fortunately, I speak female. It's long been a talent due to my appreciation of the species. I return with the blanket and three bungee cords. We wrap Kevin's body and secure it so that we can carry it to the car.

With no water left in it, Kevin's husk is light. Gillian takes his feet but doesn't need to carry much weight. I could carry him alone, but he's taller than I could manage easily.

Robert walks along beside us, the single mourner to our midnight pallbearing. After a silent trip back to the house with Gillian driving, she and I take the body to the cellar to wait for Natalie's inspection.

ALTHOUGH SHE DOESN'T admit to still being unsteady from yesterday's self-administered bout of sweating sickness, Natalie accepts the stool I pull over to the workbench so that she can get off her feet. She undresses the body with a no-nonsense air to take a closer look and sets the scorched clothing aside. She's thorough and professional.

She inspects him visually for a moment, then cuts into Kevin's desiccated abdomen with a scalpel, hmmm-ing and ah-ing. Her attitude is clinical until she grabs an arm to turn him, and it cracks out of the socket, tearing away in a small shower of dust.

"Jumpin' jujubees!" She sets the arm aside. It trails dust and flakes as it goes. "Don't mention that to Robert." She smirks at me conspiratorially. The incident appears to have perked her up. "You look a little green, there, Tom."

"Seems more real right now than it did last night. And way more ghoulish." I bring my hand to my nose, but I can't wipe away the musty smell released when the arm broke free. I'm more than a little grossed out by the thought that I've just breathed in a little bit of Kevin.

"It's time to cover him back up, anyway. I haven't learned anything. Basically, he's been drained. Every drop of essence is just gone. Nothing at all lingers. It would usually take a few days for the last sniff of it to leave a body. He's a blank. It's like he was never there."

We wrap him back up in the blanket, and Natalie takes my arm as we head upstairs. I'm just not sure who's steadying who.

***

There are only nine left now from the full coven of eighteen to lend our strength to any magic to come.

Natalie silently takes stock of the available assets as she looks from face to face in Robert's living room at the magical folk who remain.

Me? I barely count as a magical contributor. Even before Eunice bound my magic, I wasn't much of a warlock. The only thing magic about me is my ability to shift, and I needed a few drops of Cassie's blood to gain control of that. Any magic I have now is borrowed.

I have a strong male essence, though. Gillian assures me of that, although it sounds like an accusation the way she says it. In this aging-itself-out-of-existence coven town, only Robert, Darrin, and I are left to provide the essential whiff of testosterone to keep balance.

At the moment, Robert's barely functional. Back in the day, me and my buddies would have written off his expressions of grief as unmanly. We would have told him to buck up, get a grip. Or just avoided him until he could hold it together. Times change. I know better now. Since the night he prevented Kevin from touching magical objects so he couldn't abuse his gift, he has shown me over and over again what it means to be a man.

Natalie encourages the guests who were participants in Anat's ritual to talk about what happened. The first to speak, Prudence, holds tight to Sarah's hand.

"I can tell what I remember, but it's patchy," Prudence says, her voice wavering. "I wanted us to stay. We haven't missed a full moon together since we met. Cassie said she was drawing the Goddess down, but the goddess never acted like that before. She named herself—said she's called Anat. And then she…dear Goddess." Prudence starts to cry quietly and leans into Sarah for comfort.

"And the fertility ritual," Jane adds quickly, avoiding looking at Robert. He wouldn't see her anyway because his swollen eyes are hidden by the hands which cradle his down-turned head. "It was weird. I'm afraid for her daughter if Maureen puts that teddy under her bed. It jumped around like something from The Exorcist."

Nat takes a noisy swig of water from the water bottle at her right hand before she speaks. She spent the night at the hospital and then discharged herself to get back to business. I gotta give it to her, she's a trooper. But she isn't up to snuff right now. She looks exhausted.

"Nat, I think it's best if Gillian leads for now." I hand her another bottled water to replace the empty one. "You're too weak."

She takes another swig and purses her lips, then says, "Yes, and I'm too tainted by my more gray-area experimentations to feel comfortable fighting something that clearly draws its magic from the darkness anyway." She rubs her eyes with the back of her hand and you can see she's fighting a yawn. "When I thought we were dealing with Eunice, I was sure I could beat the rancid old biddy. But not now. Gillian's the only one of us who's managed to keep herself away from darker temptations over the years."

"Have I?" Gillian shakes her head. "When Martin got sick..."

"You what? You lit selfish candles, hoping he'd live? You cursed the goddess for turning her face away? You stopped believing for a moment he would only be stopping for a while in the Summerlands?"

Gillian's eyes close softly, but her face is impassive. She opens them again and a line of moisture glimmers on the top of her lower eyelids. "Yes. I called on the Goddess, I begged her to allow him to live. And I got angry when she didn't heal him. I procured some things I'm not proud of. I came close to using them."

Natalie pats her hand. "But you didn't use them, did you?" Gilly shakes her head. "What you did wasn't dark, dear. I'm sure the Goddess has forgiven you for being only human."

Everyone knows Natalie doesn't believe. She's an atheist pagan who sees the Goddess as a euphemism for the magical force in nature. That's not a problem here: the witchery in Giles has always been eclectic. The words don't mean much coming from her, but none of the ardent believers in the circle disagree when she continues.

"You're the cleanest of us. You would have been high priestess if you had accepted the coven's offer. And that's why you'll need to lead whether or not Tom thinks I'm up to snuff."

Gillian looks around the room wistfully. "If that's true, then Goddess help us all. We've wandered so very far from where we started."

I shove the big couch and coffee table into a corner of the room so that we can form a close circle. Natalie settles onto the couch after offering

Gillian a crystal ball. She soon closes her eyes. Good. She needs to rest.

Gillian arranges us.

"Tom, you take the quarter. Janice, you across from Winifred—oldest and youngest just so." She sorts us all into our positions efficiently.

The locals know to stay away from "Natalie the Gypsy Queen" at the annual Witching Faire because Nat has no talent for telling the future. She does, however, have a well-developed talent for finding "lost" items her patrons somehow left behind. But the crystal itself, like all crystal, is a true conduit for magic. Gillian places it in the center of the circle where we all now sit cross-legged, except for Winifred, whose ancient knees no longer easily bend that way. She perches instead on a kitchen chair.

Gillian takes the hands of the witches on either side of her. She has always had the talent to see behind the locked doors of the past and sometimes, of the future. But she never liked it. She avoided it. Said it wasn't right to push into someone's life that way.

Hands raise and grasp now all around the circle. Although I can no longer feel magic, I'm sure it flows through me, picking up some of my essence and contributing it to the flow.

She begins the chant. The golden candles around the colorless globe flare as the power streams around the circle. The candles are the good ones, the ones that contain some of the noble metal rather than being colored completely by a substitution. The radiance is nothing like the lights that the Cassie-thing raised the night before, but it sure feels like a nod from the Goddess that the prayer was heard.

I never take my eyes off the picture that develops in the globe. On a throne sits a woman in an Egyptian robe and headdress. Next to her, a man dressed in nearly the same attire. And before them, hundreds, on their knees, their foreheads touching the floor.

Gillian speaks, but her voice is hushed. "This is no demon. At least not as I understand demons to be. This is worship. Organized religion. I think Cassie was right—we're dealing with a goddess."

Then, the picture in the globe changes and the body of the woman from the throne is being wrapped in cotton strips and placed within a sarcophagus. Natalie sits up, immediately alert, and pulls a small sketchbook from beneath her robe. She sketches as many of the symbols that are engraved on the lid as she can before the flash of history in the crystal is gone. Too soon, the images fade. We've seen all that will be seen tonight.

"Thank you, Goddess, for what has been revealed." Gillian lets go of the hands that hold to hers and steps back from the circle.

I go straight from witch mode to detective mode. "Does anyone know what the symbols mean?"

Heads shake in the negative. Natalie says, "It was definitely Egyptian. The class I took in costume and fashion design in college was years and years ago, but I've got a good memory for that kind of thing." She holds up her drawing. "These are the symbols as close as I can capture them."

I take the drawing and study it. "That's it exactly."

"Do you recognize them?"

I reply, "I do know a few hieroglyphs, but I don't know these."

Robert contributes more than a nod for the first time since Gillian and I carried his son's body to the basement the night before. "I know someone who can help. I have a friend at the University who's an expert in Egyptology. I'll take the drawings into Boston tomorrow and see if I can get us some information."

"Are you sure?" I ask. I don't think he's ready to take an active part in this.

"Yes. Yes, it will keep my mind occupied."

I start to move the furniture back into place. "If you're feeling up to it, then I guess that's it. If everyone could leave at random intervals like you did when you got here so that it doesn't look like we've been together, that would be great."

The group breaks up, parting more solemnly than usual as group members leave every ten to fifteen minutes.

Robert nurses a whiskey, lost in his own thoughts.

I grab a blanket from the linen closet and cover Natalie on the couch. Her snoring is quiet, but persistent. She's not going anywhere tonight.

I walk Gillian to the door. When I return, Robert has moved to the study. I signal him good night on the way to my room. I think about stopping to keep him company for a while, but I know what's on his mind, and what could I say? There was no love lost between Kevin and I. I continue down the hall.

I won't be going out the window tonight. The danger is too close, too real. How in the world can this small group of mostly old biddies, two old roosters, and whatever I am, challenge a being who drained the life out of a man with nothing more than a full moon and a small circle of elderly witches?

I stop a moment, think about going back to Robert. He's offered me nothing but support since Eunice took Cassie. I should be able to offer him mine in his grief. Kevin wasn't much of a legacy to leave, but he's the one that Robert had.

But I can't do it. It was only a month ago that Kevin grabbed Cassie outside the shop and threatened her, terrified her.

No, I can't say I'm sorry that he's dead. Not even to comfort a friend.

***

"Robert?"

He raises his head, his eyes not focusing fully for a moment.

"Tom. I must have fallen asleep." He looks at the empty glass his hand still cradles on the side table. "I guess I had a little more to drink than my doctor would advise."

I shrug. "No one would blame you. I just thought...well, I was on my way to the bathroom and I thought you'd be uncomfortable in the morning if you stayed in the chair overnight."

Robert stands, and I turn to leave, but I turn back when he says my name quietly. I turn and look into his red-rimmed eyes, then look away, uncomfortable as always with emotion.

"Tom, I wanted to say...I know Kevin earned your dislike, but..."

I cut him off. I can't deal with this. Soppy man emotion—no way. I do my best to sound adult about it. "Robert, I can't imagine what it feels like to lose a son. I don't know what to say to you." I pause to push back the selfish worry that's beginning to surface. "I'd understand if you didn't want me around right now."

"No, Tom. This doesn't change anything. I was

going to tell you that I'll do my best to put aside my pain and stay focused on this so that we don't lose Cassie, too." His voice breaks, then he regains control. "Cassie's a good girl. Kevin was…damn it, you know what he was. But I was only starting to come to grips with that. I'd hoped, with time…"

I dip my eyes, ashamed that I was only thinking of me.

"The box, Tom. Did you get close enough to see the box?"

"Yeah, it…" And then a flash of memory comes to me, pictured the way that Cat sees the world. "It could have been the twin of the one Eunice put in the attic, except it was a little bigger, I think, and it was painted differently. But it had the same symbols Eunice taught me: life, death, rebirth."

"So, it's a box to preserve him somehow? She preserved Kevin's life?" His expression turns suddenly hopeful.

"I don't think so, man." His expression falls again. "I don't mean to be harsh, but don't get your hopes up. What she did to him wasn't gentle. I'm pretty sure she used him for something the box needed."

Robert sits back down, and I take the chair across from him, leaning forward onto my arms, working to bring the fuzzy cat memory of the box into focus. "Cat saw something once that didn't really register with me at the time. Probably because I was more focused on the bedspread fringe than on what Eunice was doing. But I saw her take a box out of the heating vent above her bed a few months ago."

"So, that was the box she had when…"

"No, that was the one she took to the attic. The one that got Cassie. When she came back from the attic, she looked almost joyous, despite having to lay down almost immediately, saying she felt ill." I don't mention it was probably due to a little something extra in her tea that made her weak and sick after a meeting with Kevin.

"How does that help us?"

"Well, first, it helps us by pointing out that I'm a jerk for not remembering it sooner. Because if she's hiding the boxes in the house, I bet that's where she put them. I could have had them the first time I went there, I could have…."

I stop myself: bad timing. I don't need to tell Robert that if I'd latched onto Cat's memory sooner his son might still be alive. What do they say? Hindsight is 20/20? "I have to get in there again. Because I think I know where to look." I stand and lean over, put my hand on his shoulder. "I'm doing this for Cassie, but I'm also doing it for you now, to help you avenge Kevin."

He still looks rough when he answers, but his voice is stronger, calmer. "I could lure her away from the shop again. We just need a better plan than last time. I couldn't hold her interest long enough."

"We need to get her farther away so she can't get back so fast." I snap my fingers with a flourish and finish the move with a well-executed point. "You know what she really wants, right?"

"Other than to destroy us all?"

"She wants me."

I can tell he's surfin' my waves when the corners of his mouth turn up in a faint, sad smile.

FROM BEHIND A SHELTERING trash can, I watch Robert and the Cassie-thing shove a set of large bags into the back hatch of his SUV. "Thanks, Cass. I feel a hundred years old since they discovered Kevin's body. I'm useless. I can't believe I have to have a tiny girl help me with my packages. Sorry I couldn't find a spot on the other side of the street."

The thing that calls herself Anat smiles her version of a Cassie-smile. It never touches her eyes. It barely moves her stolen lips. "Think nothing of it. It must be so difficult for you. Was he your only child?"

"He was. His mother died shortly after he was born. I never remarried." Robert's face falls with true grief. I hate putting him through this.

159

He watches Cassie walk back across the street to the shop and waits until she hits the sidewalk to call to her, "Cass, by the way. I'm planning a remembrance, something simple. I hope you'll attend?" His hand rests on the pop-up hatch, ready to close it.

She turns and calls back, a look of annoyance showing plainly on her face until she manages to hide it, "Sure, I'll be there. Just let me know."

That's my cue. The Cassie-thing's eyes are drawn by Cat when I dart out from behind my shelter, dash down the sidewalk, and leap easily into the back of the vehicle behind Robert's back just before he slams the hatch shut. In the same smooth gesture, he slides a set of headphones up over his ears and heads quickly for the driver's side door which he'd left open for a fast escape. It goes just as smooth as when we'd rehearsed it. An unusual amount of traffic roars across her path as Anat tries to get to the SUV before Robert drives away. The choir members do a great job running interference. It's like a used-car ballet.

Finally, she runs into the street with her hand held up against the traffic and the driver of the car barely manages to stop as the one behind rear-ends it, causing it to slide forward a foot before it halts inches away from her.

Too late. Robert's SUV is moving. I stretch up

and press Cat's paws against the back window so I
can look her right in the face as it goes.

***

Robert's car flies around the corner where the
road ends at Giles Woods, tires beneath it squealing,
then he flings open the car door so Cat can dart out.
I get to the tree line, where I turn and watch him
slam the door and peel out, headphones still on his
head, and his eyes searching the rear view mirror for
Cassie's vehicle. It should have taken the Cassie-
thing only a few minutes to get to the back of the
shop and start out after him.

Natalie had applied a magical limiter to Cassie's
economy car only that morning. The best "Cassie"
is going to be able to do in it is 55 miles an hour,
but the thing inside of Cassie has no way of
knowing that isn't the usual speed the car can
achieve. Eunice had never driven it. Eunice had, in
fact, seldom driven at all, not even the well-
maintained station wagon from the seventies she'd
kept parked behind the shop and sometimes had her
staff use for deliveries.

Robert will step it up to 56 miles per hour when
he sees Cassie's car rounding the corner behind him.
It should be easy for him to stay in sight so that she
can follow him, but with the headset still on his
head, he won't have to respond if she honks her
horn or tries to signal him some other way. If he

manages to lose her and can't get her back by slowing down, he'll shoot me off a text. There are things that could go wrong, but at least helping me plot it all out had perked Robert up.

When I see Cassie's car pass me, I head through the woods on my way back to town. I push back the image of Cassie, furious, at the wheel. That isn't Cassie.

But it will be.

I SWEAR CAT IS GRINNING as he looks out the back window of Robert's SUV. Taunting me, daring me to catch him.

I race to the back of the house and back into the alley, then zoom along with the gravel showering out from under my wheels. When I get to the cross street, I lay on the horn and drive straight through without stopping. Wheels squeal to the side but my course stays true. When a horn blares, I raise a hand from the wheel to give the other driver a very human, one-finger salute.

After I turn the corner where the road runs out at the edge of Corey Woods heading toward the freeway to Boston, Robert is right in front of me. I'll be able to catch him, even if he makes it to the highway before I do.

Damn this car! I'm hitting top speed at fifty-five miles per hour? I'd have been better off with Eunice's antique. Robert is just far enough in front of me that I can't get his attention. I lay on the horn, but he's wearing some headset contraption. He's oblivious. I've got the pedal to the floor, but this piece of junk doesn't respond.

Finally! A full hour outside of Giles and nearly past Boston, he exits the freeway to pull into a gas station and park at a pump. I roll into the bay behind him. He's got his headset off now, and I call to him as he heads into the station to pay.

He looks surprised to see me. "Oh, hello Cass. I didn't know you were traveling today, too. I'm headed for Hartford. You?"

"I was following you." I try to work my lips into a friendly smile, but I know they're tight with anger. "I tried to get your attention back in Giles, but you didn't notice. Cat jumped into your SUV just before you took off. I need to get in there. He's been gone a long time. I was afraid if he got out at the end of your trip, I'd never see him again."

Robert cocks his head to the side and raises an eyebrow. "Oh, that was Cat? I'm sorry, I had no idea. I let him out before I left Giles. I would have returned him to you if I'd known. There are so many black cats around town. The blasted thing crawled right up in the front seat and startled the bejesus out of me."

"Where exactly did you let him out?"

"Just on the edge of Corey Woods. Close to the road leading to the choir grounds. I'm sure he'll come home soon."

I don't have time for his platitudes. I need to get back to Giles and Corey Woods. I hustle back and peel out of the station as fast as this rotten car will let me.

FEW WOULD NOTICE the arc of blue sparks that leap from Gillian's fingertips to the doorknob as she reaches for it and turns. What had been locked is now unlocked, and I slip through, giving her a wink as she heads off in the other direction, her part in our caper done for now.

With Natalie's skinny keister settled on the bench in the front of the store, and Gillian keeping lookout from a hidden spot in the backyard of the store next door, we've got every approach covered. Nat's prepared with concerns about tainted teas to delay Eunice if she returns unexpectedly, and there's no way I'm dropping my phone this time.

I travel quickly to Eunice's bedroom, hoping I'm right about where I'll find the box. When I get there, I realize I haven't got anything to remove the screws from the vent cover. I'm a screw-up. A spaz. All the planning, and I can't get a tiny detail like this right.

No, the lingerie drawer. I always wondered why she left a screwdriver there. I rush to the dresser, and there it is. Still a creature of Eunice's habits.

I bolt back across the room, climb on the headboard, and twist away the screws. I have to hunch slightly while I work because I'm too tall to stand up straight on the headboard shelf, but I can see something shoved into the vent. I can't help but ask for a small blessing: dear Goddess, let it be what we need to get my Cassie free.

With the screws removed and safely stowed in my jeans pocket, I pry the vent off and look inside. It's not even a real vent, it's just a storage space. There are two boxes there, the one I'd seen before in the attic, and a similar one in brighter colors that has to be the one I'd seen at the ritual grounds. They sit side by side.

I grab for one of them. It takes me a moment to react to the pain when the surface of the box goes from room temperature to intense heat in an instant. Then, instinct kicks in, and I pull my hand back, putting my burned fingers in my mouth to wet them and put out the fire. It doesn't help much. A more expressive man would scream.

Not good. I look back into the vent and the box has a definite glow about it, a warning. The other box looks dull. I have to try. I risk the unburned fingers on my left hand with a quick touch. They come away without further injury. Throwing caution to the wind, I grab the box and pull it out of the vent. The other box is obviously active in some way that this one is not.

I tuck it into the canvas bag slung over my shoulder and try to focus on a plan B for the other box through the haze of throbbing pain that keeps biting down on my fingers.

I haul ass to the kitchen and dig into the back of one of the drawers for an oven mitt. It's an older, worn one that Eunice and I hadn't used for quite a while. The chance of her noticing it missing is small.

I get back up to the bedroom and the box has stopped glowing, but I'm not taking any chances. I grasp the box in the mitt, and the surface starts to glow again with heat. The mitt starts to smoke. It's not going to work. I pull it back out of the vent and spit on the smoldering glove to stop the burn, then shove it into my bag to remove the evidence. I'm out of ideas on how I can grab the box without alerting Eunice when she returns. Tongs? No. I could probably grab it fine, but if it will burn the mitt, it will burn the bag when I put it in there. And who knows what else will happen if I get it out of here? For now, it stays.

I've at least got the one. That has to be worth something.

I replace the vent and screws with my clumsy

but unburned left hand. It's an effort, but I manage.

I slip down the stairs for my getaway.

And then slip quickly back up to move the screwdriver from the nightstand back to the lingerie drawer.

I nearly gave myself away.

***

"All right, Tom?" Gillian asks, as I walk toward her, hanging on tight to the canvas bag I wear cross-body over my shoulders. I don't care if Eunice does show up. I'm not letting go until it's safely stored someplace she'd never think to look. I keep my burned hand hidden because I don't want anything to distract Gillian from our plan. It's difficult, though, because it still feels like I'm toasting my fingers on a stick for s'mores.

"Yeah, I'm good. Let's get Nat and go. I have to get back to take care of something after we drop this off." I keep my burned hand curled in so that she can't see the redness and blisters.

After Gillian checks that the coast is clear up front, we walk out of the alley and pick up Nat, then continue along the street to the Giles Gallery of Modern Art, where we quickly step inside. Dash Simmons, the proprietor, locks the door behind us and we hustle in.

"Come along, come along," he says, leading us into a back room. Once there, he lifts up the end of an area rug, exposing a pull ring in the wooden floor. He pulls up and a hatch opens, revealing a narrow staircase. The stairs are lit with a series of small inset lights at each step.

"Well, go down, if you're going," he urges. "I don't want the entrance exposed any longer than necessary."

I go first and the others follow behind. Simmons comes down last, flipping on a light switch near the top of the stairs before he pulls the hatch closed.

At the bottom of the stairs, we enter a small, cement chamber. Simmons skims by us, close to the wall, to get around in front and input the door code to unlock the heavy steel door that is the only feature of the room.

The door opens on a larger room with one small easel in the center. A comfortable-looking recliner chair sits directly in front of it. I've been here once before as Cat when I was spying for Eunice. Dash had no idea that letting a friendly cat into the cellar would cause him so much trouble. Just another one of the things I did for Eunice that I feel guilty about. Of course, he has no idea what it cost him.

"Oh my...is that?" Gillian asks.

"It most definitely is! The yellows and the greens, those bold strokes!" Nat exclaims. She moves up close to the painting. "During the war, I presume?"

"Yes. My family should have given it back when

it was all over, but..." He shrugs. "No one can get in here. The walls are too thick. When Robert called to arrange this, he said he'll forgive my debt if I let you stow your item here. I could own my gallery outright again. And none of you will tell about the painting?"

I nod. "I know it's hard to believe, but Robert...yes, he'll deed it back to you after we pick the box up. He's already signed the transfer papers and put them into his safety deposit box at the bank in case anything happens to him before that time arrives. And you have my word for all of us, too. This room stays a secret."

I remove the precious box from my bag and set it down on the reading table that sits next to the viewing chair. "There," I say. "That's what we need to protect."

Simmons eyeballs the box for a moment. "Egyptian. Quite old. Not my era, mind you. But an interesting piece. Fired clay? It should be fine in the vault. It was built for only one item, but it's temperature and moisture regulated."

"And warded as of early this morning," Natalie adds.

"Yes, and warded, whatever that means. I assume it has something to do with the mysterious city choir I've always done my best not to know too much about." He motions toward the door to shepherd us out. "If you absolutely need to access it, you can contact me at home or at the shop. But I won't have all of you going in and out all the time. Do you hear? I won't have it."

He glances anxiously at the painting, being a good mother hen to his illicit chick. His mini-Dali mustache trembles at the corners. I'm sure he anticipates a flock of visitors day and night now that we know what's down here, but the last thing anyone wants is Eunice noticing that any member of our little gang has suddenly developed an unusual interest in art.

I do my best to reassure him, working to control my voice as my fingers throb. "You've got nothing to worry about. We'll be back one time, and when we come for it, there have to be at least two of us on the phone call—and Robert is included in the group. Same thing for when we arrive to pick it up. If only one of us calls or shows, or anyone else is with us, you don't know what the hell he or she is talking about. And never, I mean never, mention it to Cassie. Or anybody else for that matter. And me? You don't even know me, man."

His mustache stops quivering as he nods his head. That's good. Because he can't be walking around anxious. Eunice always had a way of sniffing out when someone was hiding something. I'll bet that spider sense followed Eunice right into Cassie's body instead of dying with her.

"Just one more thing. We need a couple of pictures of the box before we go." I pull the phone Gillian insists I carry out of my back-pocket with my good hand, but it will take both of them to manage a photo. I fumble with buttons for a while, my blistered fingers shooting streams of agony up my arm as I try to figure out how to turn the camera on, but it's a blasted mystery. I'll never get why modern folks need to carry an entire Sears electronics department around with them. I curse the device out firmly but softly under my breath.

Natalie pulls her own camera-phone out of her bag. "For crying out loud, Tom. Stop being such an old fuddy and join the 21st century." She has the pictures sorted out quickly, photographing it from all sides. When she's done, she taps at it for a few more minutes and announces, "There. Off to everyone's email."

We don't open the box. The last thing we need is to set off a curse we aren't prepared for.

We follow Dash back up the stairwell. We're unusually silent as we tramp upwards. Nat and Gillian aren't quibbling, and despite being right behind me, Nat isn't even commenting on the fit of my jeans. No reason for celebration yet, I guess. We have the box, but we have no idea exactly *what* we have.

With its fitted hatch and attached oriental carpet back in place, Dash makes the entry to the hidden vault disappear as tidily as any witch's spell could have done.

Outside, I finally show Gillian my burns and ask her if she can do something for them. She gasps, then asks, "What happened?"

"Later. I need to shift to stop the pain. I can't bear it much longer. I'll head through the woods to give Cat a little reward for good behavior during his part in this caper. Look for me at your place in an hour or so."

I leave my clothes on the ground in the narrow yard beside the gallery and she bags them before she carries them to her car. I'd exchanged the smaller pain of Cat's sore foot for the pain of the burns, but Cat's not even favoring his other legs anymore. Compared to what I'm escaping, it's nothing.

As I dart down the street and off to the woods, I know the box is safer than anything else in this town. Dash is the last guy Eunice would suspect of hiding anything, and Robert is expert with wards. Yes, that box is much safer than any one of us if that body-stealing demon figures out what we've done.

I WATCH GILLIAN SOAKING strips of gauze in a brown mixture from my perch outside the kitchen window. I know it's wrong to observe her this way, but I like to see her like this—content, active, exactly as I pictured she would be when we were old together. Except I screwed that up big time. I didn't get old, and I didn't stay loyal to Gillian.

Soon enough, I give a hearty yowl to get her attention and she walks through the mud room and opens the back door for me. Cat struts in, stretching as he goes, and rubs against her leg through the Indian fabric of her long skirt. He's in a good mood after a quick but successful hunt.

"Knock it off! You'll cover me with cat hair. Your clothes are in the guest room. Come back down to the kitchen when you're dressed."

Cat makes one more long, insistent sweep of his head against her leg. "Go on now, scat!" Have I said Cat often has a mind of his own?

When I return, holding my hand out in front of me so that it doesn't brush against anything that might send the pain shooting up my arm again, she sits me down at the kitchen table and inspects my wounds. "These burns are deep. How did it happen?"

"There was a second box that reacted when I tried to grab it. That's why I left it behind."

"And you kept it to yourself because you've suddenly grown fond of pain?"

"Because I didn't want to distract you. This is about Cassie, not about me."

She winds wide strips of gauze around each of my burned fingers in turn, being careful not to hurt me more than she has to. Healing is one of the first things most witches want to learn when they find out about magic. Not me. I never did. I was too busy figuring out how to use magic for pleasure. Gillian always thought of others first.

For my part, I suck it up. I've already experienced Cat's painful death six times. Blistered burns? They're nothin'. But I'm kind of glad she isn't trying to have a conversation while she works, because I'm pretty sure my voice would waver and break if I tried to use it. Because, oh man, blistered burns? Intense.

When she's done, she bends down and kisses

the back of my hand gently, in a motherly way, on one of the few spots that isn't bandaged. "There, that's the bit that actually makes it all better. The herbal soak is just for show." She looks up at me, smiling. "Tom, I really am glad you and Cassie found each other. You could have run. Hell, if it was me forty years ago, you would have run."

I cut her off. "You can't believe that. Do you really believe I didn't love you enough to fight for you?"

"No. I know you loved me. But back then that would never have stopped you from running away, just like you ran to Eunice when you got scared about settling down and starting a family."

And I know she's right. I ran, I cheated, I lied. I kept my feelings bottled up so tight that I might as well not have had any. I was a perfect servant for Eunice: I'm a much better cat than I am a man. I pretend to inspect her handiwork, directing my attention to my bandages.

"What I mean to say, Tom, is…you've changed. It's too bad you didn't get to where you are half a lifetime earlier, but I've told you before—I got my Marty out of that deal, and I wouldn't have given him up for anything. Looks like we both earned our second chances. So…let's get over to Robert's and see what he's found out about that box, so we can see about getting Cassie her second chance, too."

***

Robert moves faster than usual as he leads us toward the study, appearing not to notice the arthritis that slows him down most days. Natalie is already there waiting. Gillian's eyes narrow, but Nat just gives her a happy smile. There's something odd going on between those two, but I don't need to get myself in the middle of some senior spat.

Robert's face is more animated than it's been since Kevin was killed.

"You're not going to believe this. The writing on the box basically says 'this is the place of Anat.' Yes, the goddess Anat. Believed to be the consort of the god Ba'al. Loved the battlefield. Dangerous."

"So we're dealing with a goddess, just like Cassie said?" Gillian's head bobs rhythmically for a few beats as she takes in the information. "That makes sense. We call on the Goddess for our magic and healing. And now we've got one on our doorstep. Just not the one we were expecting."

My hands clench as I listen to her talk. Great. Not just some horny old witch come back to life, but a goddess of unknown power. I can't deal with this. I unclench my fists when I realize I'm in pain, and the angry red marks where my fingernails cut into my palms slowly ease.

Robert blats on about goddesses this and demon that, but the stuff floating around in the sunbeam behind him is lots more interesting than most of what he's saying. It must be fascinating stuff for a guy who's spent so much of his life with his nose in dusty books researching magical history, and the ladies are hanging on his every word. But me? I need something to do.

Still...I don't want to stop him when he's acting like himself again. I sit tight while he continues, working to keep my eyes on his face.

"Perhaps that's why Ba'al had two consorts: their sister Ashtarte was the gentler of the two."

I say, "I'd rather she'd turned out to be a garden-variety demon. At least there are passages in your books that deal with demonic possession."

"Maybe it's not such a problem," Robert says.

He really needs to speed it up. I've got my eye on that sunbeam again, and there's a couple specks of dust in there that need to be knocked senseless. I prod, "And why isn't it a problem?"

"Doug also said that the entire god and goddess scene, angels and demons, they're the same thing. He believes that those beings were an ancient race. Maybe even aliens."

Okay, that's it. Done listening. "Really, man? That old chestnut? Let's just cover our heads with tinfoil hats to get rid of her."

Gillian gives me a schoolmarmy look. "Let him talk, Tom. I want to hear this."

Robert nods a thanks, but there's no reprimand in it for me. "Doug makes a compelling argument. Personally, I've never believed in a goddess, preferring to think of her as an embodiment of the power of nature." His eyes travel to Natalie, and

Gillian watches his face closely as they do. "Nat and I have always agreed on this point, although we've seldom agreed on much else. But I have no problem with those who think of the goddess anthropomorphically. It's just a way of visualizing where a witch or warlock finds power."

He shifts in his chair and crosses his leg, then puts it back on the floor with a wince. Looks like the adrenalin has worn off and his arthritis is making itself known again.

"If you think about it, it makes sense. Many of those ancient gods were real bastards. Ba'al was presented as just one of many competing gods to the god of the Hebrews. Even the old testament never denied he was a god. Later theologians did, calling him Ba'al Zeebub to demonize him, which became Beelzebub in Christian mythology. Gods, goddesses, angels, and demons. They're all the same thing. Just a long-lived, ancient race that has a closer connection to magic than we do.

Gillian stirs her tea absently. Then she says, "So, she may be a goddess, but we can approach her like she's a demon."

I smile. "I have zero problem with that. Let's get going and exorcise the wench. Robert, did your historian friend have any ideas around what the box is for?"

"The symbols are for life, death, and rebirth, as you've told us. And, of course, there are hieroglyphs which represent Anat herself. Nothing unusual there. They're typical symbols that could be found on sarcophagi, apparently. He didn't have much else to add, although he did send some links to other potential research sources."

Gillian had been tapping away on her laptop while I talked to Robert. Now, she turns the laptop so that the small TV screen faces him. "Take a look at this and tell me what it looks like to you. This is one of the sources he sent."

I lean in for a look. "This box has the same symbols." He points to them in turn. "Life, death, and rebirth." He looks up at Gillian. "I wonder if these boxes are more common than we thought and we're chasing a dead end?"

Gillian shakes her head. "No, I don't think so. This one is in a museum in Egypt. It was discovered in the 1890s. When the archeologist opened it, it contained a human heart. The expedition leader who was with him destroyed the heart because he insisted it was beating. Obviously, everyone thought he was a bit mad after that."

"Interesting. Anything on the other symbols?"

"No, not much here. I can email the museum to see if they've ever interpreted all of the symbols on the box."

I cut in. "Do it. Anything we can add to our store of knowledge is important. How do you work one of those computer things, anyway? Could I figure it out and help?"

Gillian looks at me the way she'd look at an

overeager child. "Truthfully, Tom? Nobody has time to teach you right now. I don't need a student with the attention span of a cat."

I start working up a head of steam but get off the anger train before I blow it out my smokestack. This isn't the time to get into a fight over something stupid like my pride.

Gillian adds, "I didn't mean that as an insult. It came out wrong." She gives me the I'm-sorry face with the big eyes and exaggerated frown. "I just meant that you don't really seem to like technology, and since you act like it takes a techno-mage to operate a phone, you'll really be done in by the internet."

I concede. "Sure, whatever that is. You probably have a point. I got shocked hard when I got anywhere near Eunice's computer because she didn't want me using it. At least I have an excuse."

I think for a moment about what I do have to contribute, and I realize we're going to have to break our promise to Simmons and get a look inside that box.

IT'S EASIER TO REFUSE a caller than it is to refuse someone who's standing right in front of you.

There are still lights on downstairs when we cruise up to Dash's house in Robert's big SUV. We discuss our strategy as we walk up the long sidewalk to the porch.

"I'll field this one," Robert offers. "It's just like a politician to break a promise, isn't it? He isn't going to be happy that we want to do our prohibited tramping in and out in the late evening hours."

I lift my chin to acknowledge his offer and say, "Thanks, but this is my fight. And it's my promise we're breaking. It's enough that you came along."

When Dash opens the door, peering out above the inside chain lock with a hint of an embroidered red silk robe showing through the slit, I say, "I'm sorry, Dash. We wouldn't be here if it wasn't important. We need to take another look at the item the ladies and I left at the shop."

"I knew it. I knew you'd continue to have demands. That's how it works with you people." He glares at Robert. "You said you'd let me run the shop like I always had after you took it over, but Kevin was constantly having me hide things for you. Plus having to put the prices up so you could take a cut off the top, and threatening it would go badly for me if I didn't."

I exchange another quick glance with Robert. He looks as surprised as if he'd just been slapped. I can tell he had no idea what Kevin had been doing.

Dash unchains the door and opens it wide, apparently resigned to our request. "Step in, then. I'll get dressed."

A white-haired man in a matching red robe walks into the foyer behind him with a questioning look on his face. Dash looks back at him and says, "I have to go out for a while, Jon. You might as well watch the rest of the movie. I doubt I'll be in the mood for it when I get home."

Jon shrugs and goes back to where he came from. We wait while Dash goes upstairs to change.

Still looking down the hall, I say, "I think I'm beginning to understand how you got such a bad reputation in town despite turning out to be such a solid guy."

We don't turn to each other. Guys of our

generation don't. There won't be hugs all around, but I can see his head bob slightly in acknowledgment in my peripheral vision.

The last of the guard I'd put up against the man dissolves as I realize Kevin blamed his own strong-arm stuff on his father. And I'm betting Robert had an inkling of that. My dad would have taken the hit for me while he tried to straighten me out. As far as I can tell, the only thing Robert is guilty of is being a caring father.

I really hope I'm right to trust him. If he doesn't deserve it, it could endanger Cassie. But if he does deserve it, and I don't give my trust, it could turn out just as badly.

***

It doesn't take long for the three of us to travel to the gallery and get into the vault. Dash stays upstairs at Robert's request. If all hell breaks loose, we don't want him getting caught in the demonic crossfire.

I take a deep breath, steeling myself against the possibility that opening the box will touch off a firestorm of consequences.

I use a pocket knife to pry around each side of the lid, making sure I don't hold it with the sorest parts of my wrapped fingers as I work. It's a little awkward that way, but the waxy substance that seals it cracks, and the box opens.

Nothing happens. I hear Robert's whooshing exhale behind me. He's remained so calm I didn't realize that, like me, he'd been holding his breath.

I set the lid aside so that we can see the contents. It's just like the article said: the box contains a dark, dried out lump that could definitely be a heart.

"It's not beating. I'll take that as some good luck," I say, glancing over at him.

"Yes. That may mean something. It may not." He starts taking pictures. There are symbols written on the inside as well, so he walks around the box to capture those, too.

"Could you flip the lid over, Tom? I want to see if there's anything written on the inner surface."

I do as he asks, but the lid of the box doesn't reveal more writing. It might have at one time, but the inside of it looks sooty or scorched, as though it's been subjected to fire at some point during its existence. I think about trying to brush the soot away, but I can't bring myself to touch it. There's some terrible magic involved with this, and it makes me uncomfortable being near it. I want it sealed back up as soon as possible.

It's pretty clear Robert agrees with me when he says, "Get the lid back on that thing. It gives me the willies."

***

"Can you send those to Robert's friend?" I ask Gillian in the morning after she transfers the pictures on his camera to her laptop.

Robert dials his cell as she gets to work. "Doug, got a couple more questions for you. And some pictures I think you're really going to want to see…yes, related to the Egyptian artifact."

Gillian taps away at her keyboard, then tells Robert, "Done."

"Doug, they're sent. If you could take a look and give your first impression that would be great." Robert listens then, nodding his head and interjecting a "hmmm" and a "huh" every so often as the man on the other end of the line speaks. "No, that's exactly what we need. As for a viewing—I'll ask. I don't know if the owner wants to let anyone see the find right now. Thanks, Doug. Yes, send it along when you get it. Sure, just do a reply. I'll get the info."

Robert puts his phone back into his blazer pocket and leans in onto his hands on the back of the couch, looking over Gillian's shoulder as she brings the pictures up on her laptop screen.

As he looks at the pictures, he says, "So, according to Doug, the only organ the Egyptians left in place inside the mummy was the heart. The rest of them got pickled separately and placed in jars near the sarcophagus."

"Gross. But, they used canopic jars like the ones Eunice sold for pet funerals, right?" I ask.

"Yes. Now we know why Eunice had a weakness for them."

"But why did they leave the heart in?"

"Vessel of the soul, Doug says. They believed removing the heart would cause the body to arrive in the afterlife soulless."

"What we locked up under the gallery was made to hold Anat's soul?"

Robert nods. "It's looking like that."

"So all we have to do is destroy the heart, and we destroy Anat!" I gesture a little too enthusiastically and spill my tea. Great timing. I leap up and head for the kitchen for paper towels, calling over my shoulder, "Then that's it. Because I would be happy to rip that nasty lump of gristle apart with my own two hands. We'll go after I clean up this mess."

The two of them continue murmuring as I walk away, but I can't hear them from the kitchen. When I get back and start soaking up the spilled tea, Gillian says, "We don't think it's going to be as simple as destroying the heart, Tom. If the heart is just a vessel and she's not in there, then Cassie is her vessel now. We'd have to get Anat's essence back into the box before we destroy the heart."

My own heart sags. "Damn. That's why it wasn't beating. No one's home. Of course it couldn't be that easy." I finish sopping up the mess and take the wad of wet towels out to the kitchen trash. I stand there for a minute, looking down into the silver trashcan with its lid standing open to all the trash of the day. Everything we learn is just another dead end. None of it brings me closer to having Cassie in my arms again. I move my foot and the lid falls with a thunk.

When I head back to the living room, my burned hand brushes against the doorway. I wince against the sudden pain. The burn. What was different about the other box? And then it hits me. "Do you think the reason the other box burned me when I tried to pick it up is because it's inhabited?"

Gillian's eyes flit away from mine, and she turns back to sit forward on the couch as my question ends. It hangs there in midair until I sit in the chair across from her and she quietly answers, still not looking at me. "Cassie told you what Eunice had planned, I mean she said it, that Eunice has plans for you and that box. Robert and I think...if that second box contains Ba'al's heart...well, why else would she be so concerned about getting Cat back if not that she needs you...your body?"

"Of course she does." I stand up and circle them as what that means hits me. "I mean, why not? Two weeks ago I was almost back to a semblance of a normal human life. But then some randy Egyptian goddess steals my girlfriend. And why wouldn't she want to stick her dead lover-boy in me? Because that's just the wacky kind of life I lead." The old me, the selfish Tom finds his opening and takes over. "I used to think that I got what I deserved for cheating on you, Gillian, when Eunice stuffed me into a cat, but I'm not sticking around for this."

I can be out of town before the sun comes up tomorrow. I bolt out of the room and run to the kitchen door, not even bothering to close it so I can shift and disappear into the night.

I don't even get ten feet out before I realize that the Tom who runs away isn't me anymore. I have someone to stay for. Someone who needs me. Someone I love more than myself.

I turn and lope back to the house. Gillian is just closing the door as I slink back in. I'm not proud of my impulse, but at least I can hold my tail high instead of between my legs.

Whoever that Tom was, I'm done with him.

I STEP ONTO THE headboard of my red-silk-clad bed and remove the vent cover. With Ba'al so near now, I think of him more and more. This silly modern life is meaningless. I long for him. But soon, very soon, I will gift him his new home and the entire world will be ours again.

I reach in for the boxes, but my hand explores farther than I need to and pulls Ba'al's box out first. Mine should have been on that side. I stand on tiptoe and peer into the vent for the box's mate.

It's gone.

My Ab Khr is gone.

The scream keens out of me into the night-time

silence of downtown Giles as I crumple to my knees.

***

Gillian is even more of a nightmare at seven in the morning than she is later in the day. With her hair down and a flowery, summer-weight robe barely covering her bulk, she looks like a garden threw up on her. She's blank for a moment when she sees me, then gives me a broad smile. I'd like to slap it off her face.

"Cass, what a nice surprise. Come in, I'll pour us some coffee." She leads me into the living room and flaps a hand toward the couch. "Take a seat, take a seat. I'll be right back out."

"Thank you," I say, trying to sound friendly but knowing I sound stiff instead. How do these people manage all that bright, yappy joy? "I just stopped by to see if you'd heard anything around town about any thefts—other than Natalie and her sleight of hand, of course. It seems that my shop was broken into again yesterday."

"Really, sweetheart?" She bustles back into the room, hands me a cup of coffee, and pushes the sugar and cream across the coffee table to me. "Was it very bad?"

"Of course it was bad! Can there be a good break in? The thief took something of my grandmother's that was precious to her. Something that would probably be of great interest in the local community—you know what I mean…something that could place the thief in grave danger if he or she attempted to use it in the wrong way."

"Well, that certainly doesn't sound good, does it? But I thought you'd cleared out Eunice's darkest magical items."

"Yes, well, there were some special items left in the attic. I was researching them. To have this come up missing—I wonder if you'd keep your ears open and ask around. I wouldn't be the least surprised to find out that Robert or Natalie had gone prowling through the house looking for anything of Eunice's they could turn to their own use."

She purses her lips and taps them with a forefinger as she rests her chin on her hand. "I'm sure it's not Nat. She's barely recovered from that bug she had earlier in the week. Plus, it's not really her style—she's more of an impulse shopper." She smiles at her own joke about Natalie's thievery. She continues when I don't respond, "And Robert? He's been very distracted since his son's death. I can't imagine him getting himself together enough to go prowling around your shop to inventory Eunice's things. What was it exactly? I'd be better able to keep an eye out for it if I knew what I was looking for."

I glare at her. "I'm just saying it could be very dangerous for whoever might have it. If you know who it is, they need to return it immediately."

She leans back in her seat and her eyes widen in response to my anger. This friendly visit is veering into unfriendly territory, and I need her to spread the word and report back to me like she would to Cassie. I reign my anger in and say, in what I hope is a soothing tone, "I'm sorry. I'm just so...worried about what could happen with such a dangerous relic." I force my face into an expression of concern. It's uncomfortable. I don't like it. But I freeze it there anyway. "I completely wouldn't want to see anyone be hurt." There, that's the kind of insipid thing Cassie would say.

Gillian's face softens. "Oh sweetheart, of course. I understand. I'll definitely ask around. Although, if I just drop it into Nat's ear, the word will spread through the gossip network before the end of the day, no matter how poorly she's doing."

"Good. Thank you." I stand to leave, but as I do, I notice a black filament on her tasteless 80s rose-print couch. I tweeze it up between my thumb and forefinger for a closer look. "This is a black cat hair."

"Is it?" she returns.

The muscles in my forehead tighten as I scrutinize her. "Are you hiding Cat from me?"

Her head shifts forward as her brow pulls down, deepening the lines between her eyebrows and accentuating her meaty double-chin. "Why would I hide Cat from you? That probably came in on my skirt after one of the strays down at the farmer's market rubbed up against my legs. Really, sweetheart, you seem so stressed. Is there anything I can do?"

"No. No, I'm fine. I'm just paranoid after this break in. It was upsetting to discover a stranger had gone through the house when I wasn't there. It's made me question everything."

She shows me out, grinning, clownish, the soul of innocence, but I'm going to keep a closer eye on that one. She's a fool, but she's a powerful fool.

ROBERT AND I ARE just sitting down to breakfast when my phone rings. I answer, and a long stream of anxiety pours out.

"She found one of Cat's hairs on the sofa, Tom. I don't think she believed me about the stray cat at the market. She was right there at my door at the crack of dawn, asking me to find out if someone had stolen a relic from the shop, and she was openly threatening about what would happen if it wasn't returned. She's not doing a very good job of staying in character."

"Eunice or Anat or whatever she is?"

"Yes. And she mentioned Nat and Robert by name. I have to admit I'm scared. I'm scared for all of us."

"Hang on a minute." I fumble to find the mute

button and then repeat what I'd just learned to Robert with my own suggestion for what needs to happen. I'm back on the phone quickly.

"Robert has two guest rooms and serious wards around the house that are regularly renewed. Call Nat and tell her to pack. We'll be out to pick both of you up as soon as he gets our morning coffee into travel cups."

I dress in a hooded sweatshirt despite the warm day, and Robert hands me a pair of sunglasses to complete my disguise. It's a short trip through town, but with Anat looking for someone to blame, the last thing any of us need is for her to spot me.

Gilly meets us at the back door when we pull into the drive. "Robert, your offer of a guest room is lovely, but I'm not sure I want to stay there. I may have panicked a bit."

Robert begins to respond, but I cut him off. "Okay, then. Robert, go ahead and let's just take her to the shop and deliver her straight to Anat. She doesn't want our protection."

"That level of sarcasm is unnecessary, Tom," Gillian replies.

"Is it? Then, what level *is* necessary? We're not talking about some old lady who's looking to give you a slap—we're talking about an ancient goddess-demon who thinks you may have something she wants and will do anything to get it back. I doubt she'd think twice about killing you where you stand. That you're still here means we get a chance to keep you safe. So you're going to Robert's."

"Fine," she responds, her mouth tight with that I'm-mad-but-I-also-know-you're-right expression I know far too well. "But what do I say about why Nat and I are staying there if anyone notices?"

"Robert's finally joined the free love movement and the two of you are his lovers?" I joke, but no one's laughing, and this weird look crosses both of their faces. Oh no…they can't be…

Of course not. I bat that thought away. Far away.

Robert has a sensible suggestion. "It's not unheard of for the leaders of the coven to close ranks during periods of leadership transition. We can tell people there's been a rift between the two of you over governance of the choir and that you've moved into the house while I moderate the disagreement to assure that it's resolved safely."

She sighs, then ushers me in to pick up her bag.

Nat has a few too many suitcases for a short stay, but Robert stows them in the back without a word. When she slides in next to me on the wide bench seat, a little too close for comfort, as always, we're off again. Soon we're waiting for the sliding iron gates at Robert's place to clank open. As soon as there's enough space, the SUV slides through and the gates close behind us.

Safety for now. But even with multiple wards by multiple practitioners, including, as Robert earlier informed me, a hundred-year-old shaman, who knows what a goddess is capable of?

***

I start to head up the stairs with the luggage when Robert's phone beeps. He flashes the screen at Gillian who raises her eyebrows as she reads it. He beckons to me, "Wait a minute, Tom. Put them down here for now. Doug's sent something to Gillian's email."

Gilly grabs her laptop bag from the pile and heads for the library with the rest of us trailing like a string of ducklings. "Just let me get the laptop booted up and we'll see if it's as exciting as he claims."

Natalie ensconces herself in a gigantic leather-covered chair then takes a bottle out of her purse. The smell of good whiskey fills the room when she twists off the cap. "Anyone?"

Robert goes to the sideboard and carries a tray full of delicate china tea cups over. "Fill 'em up. I, for one, could use a swig or two right now."

Gillian nods at Nat and picks up a cup once it's full. "It's about time somebody offered me something other than tea in this house."

I grab my cup and sip at it, not wanting to end up sloppy drunk after forty-five years of unexpected sobriety. I'm more of a cocktail man, but the whiskey goes down smooth. I almost begin to relax.

Gillian slants the laptop screen toward us and

we all lean in to look at what she's put up on the screen. "Okay. Hmmmm. He scanned a few pages from one of his books. Do you see the drawing of the box? It looks just like ours."

I lean closer, peering over her shoulder. "Same marks for life, death, and rebirth."

"So what's interesting," she says as she looks directly at me, "and stay focused, Tom, because you're going to be glad you did—this box was found hidden in the room of a young woman whose relatives claimed she was possessed. Happened in France, maybe five hundred years ago. She killed two of the village priests when they tried to exorcise her."

"What happened to her?"

"Even more interesting. Her family went into the countryside looking for a witch woman to help them. They no longer believed the church had anything to offer. She came and brought friends. They were able to send the spirit into an animal, a wolf, and they took the box away to destroy the heart that it contained. The young woman recovered completely and immediately and never talked crazy again."

"And?" I raise my eyebrows, waiting for Gillian to get to the point.

"There is no 'and' Tom. They drove it out. It can be done."

"It's no help unless it tells us how. We're as much in the dark as we were before."

Natalie gives me the hairy eyeball and offers me the bottle.

"Sorry." I hold up a hand to decline it. "I don't mean to get angry. I'm just tired of talking instead of doing."

Gillian says, "The point is, Tom, the knowledge exists. In France, those old covens have history with each other. I don't know why I didn't think about contacting Maryse before this, but a little networking never hurt."

Robert raises his glass to me in a toast. "To networking."

I shrug. "To networking." The tinkling clink of the cups reminds me of the shop door opening. Anyone, anything could be beyond it.

***

Gillian plops into the chair next to me in the den, where I'm practicing my newly developed ability to flip through 150 channels of TV over and over again without finding anything worth watching. "That was the strangest call. Aurelie asked a lot of questions about the situation, but when I asked her if her coven had ever heard about anything like this, she muted the phone and when she came back, she basically said that I was not to call the high priestess about this issue ever again. She sounded upset. Even a little stroppy, if you ask me."

"That's not like Aurelie. At least, not the little I know her."

"No, Tom, it's not. I would have liked to talk directly to High Priestess Maryse, but apparently it's not going to be allowed. I think Maryse knows something and doesn't want to let us in on it."

"Why would they hide anything from us? I mean, they came all the way here from France just to help me take control of my shifting."

"I know that. That's why this is so frustrating. You know how they kept telling you, 'the magic of our coven must be protected'? I think they're protecting some magic that they don't want us to know about. You know how secretive Maryse can be. She even pretended she didn't know English most of the time she was here. And, of course, Aurelie would never talk out of school. She dotes on the old priestess."

I give her what I once would have called my Tom-on-the-prowl smile. "You want me to call her? You know the chicks can't resist the ol' Tom Sanders charm. I'll have her spilling all her magical secrets, peeling off her dress, and begging me to marry her within minutes."

She laughs. "Oh, I have no doubt...but really, there's something going on there, and I don't have time to play games with them. We're just going to have to write off the idea of getting help from that direction."

Her phone rings. She looks at the screen, then

answers it, looking surprised. "Aurelie?"

She listens for less than a minute, then says goodbye.

When she looks up at me, she looks confused. "Well, that was odd. All she said was, 'It takes a goddess to fight a goddess.' And then she hung up."

I'D TRIED TO LOCATE Tom using some of the hair I found in the house, but his essence had decayed too much due to the length of time since he shed it. I should have tried again with more material to concentrate any essence that was left, but I had so many things on my mind. And, of course, the eventful trip to Egypt. It all got in the way. Now anything he's left in the house will be too old to use.

But if Gillian is lying and this hair is a recent dropout from Cat's coat, then I may be able to tease out his location, no matter how far away he's gone. I drop it into the simmering potion on the stove to amplify whatever essence is left. I talk to Ba'al, safe inside his box beside me, as I work.

"You'll love what I've picked for you, dear heart. Do you like being called that? It's one of those expressions that's nearly antiquated now in English, but given your circumstance, I think it suits you." I smirk as I crush the herb and bone meal mixture with the mortar and grind it fine, then dump it into the vile smelling stew in the stove.

"I knew when I met him that he was your perfect host. That's why I preserved him for you all these years. He looks quite aristocratic from the proper angle. He has that nose that was common among the Pharaohs and the Caesars—you know the one? They call it a Roman nose these days. A strong nose, a masculine nose."

My nether regions stir while I mix the potion, idly day-dreaming of what it will be like to have Ba'al pressed against me full length in Tom's body. It will soon be our time again, but without the interference of Astarte in our affairs.

With the potion ready, I barely let it cool before I tip my head back and take it in. It burns going down, but I barely feel it. I blink, and when my eyes flick open, I see through the eyes of a cat. The size of the cat is right, the eyes low to the ground with the view in the distinct shape of a cat's slits, the right height for a young cat, no longer quite a kitten, and I get a glance at a black paw beneath as he runs along. I need to catch his reflection so I can be sure. The extra spark in Cat's eyes distinguishes him from the other black cats in Giles.

He pads through the woods, on the prowl, and I ride along. He has no way of knowing I'm traveling with him tonight.

Just show me where he goes.

I expect him to head for Gillian's, but he squeezes through a space in the stone wall I recognize as the one that surrounds the old sheep's pasture in Giles woods. He's hunting. As he moves along, barely disturbing a blade of grass as he stalks, I catch the small movements around him as he identifies his prey. The possum's eyes glow red with the small reflected light of the moon through the trees. It's a young one, smaller than Cat. He blasts toward it as it turns to run. He entraps it with his full body wrapped around it, and his teeth move in to the back of the animal's neck for the kill. How delightful to share the hunt with such a creature. But it's over too soon as he drops it and moves on. He leaves the limp body where it falls. He's not hunting because he's hungry. He's as much a sportsman as I am.

He ends up at the small lake just outside the campsite. The campers won't be there. No swimming or boating is allowed after dark, but he sits looking out over the surface. There's a slight breeze and the ripples on the face of the water catch the reflected light of the moon, flickering on and off like tiny beacons in the dark.

It's not possible.

It's not possible!

The cat's vision blackens and when it returns, the line of sight raises to a man's height. A man's eyes look down to the muddy shoreline to a man's feet picking their way toward the water. He walks into it and glides smoothly out toward the center. There can be no mistake. Tom has found a way to unbind himself and control the shift.

I've seen enough. I release the vision and swipe with fury at the items strewn across the kitchen table from my potion-making. Jars, bowls, tins, fly off the surface and slam against the wall. I smash the ceramics on the counter. I must feel the destruction! A drawer full of tableware lands with a satisfying series of crashes when I rip it from its drawer and dash it across the room.

A faint sound catches my attention when I stop to breathe. A regular beat, increasing in volume until it's so loud it causes these human ears pain. I'd forgotten Ba'al's box was on the table. I fall to my knees and crawl across the filth to pick up the beating heart, feeling it pulse against my hands as I place it gently back in the Ab Khr. The sound subsides.

I know, dear heart, I know. We'll be together again soon. I hurriedly place the box back into the vent upstairs before I leave.

***

I leave the car in the camp parking lot and hurry down the path to the lake. When I reach it, I scan the surface for a sign of him. His head skims across the surface as he swims. He's made it so easy for me.

Cat is going to hate what happens next.

I call out to him, laughing. "Oh Tom. Bad, bad Tom."

He sees me now. I don't need to be riding along with him to know it. I hear his "oh hell" ripple outward as it turns from speech to yowl.

IT'S BEEN A WHILE since I shifted involuntarily, and I've never shifted in the water. I take the cold in through my man/cat mouth, wondering if Cat will drown as I sink below the surface in a frenzy of morphing body parts, but Cat coughs it out as he finally surfaces, his legs pumping frantically toward the nearest shore to escape the water he hates. But that way leads toward capture and away from the phone I left on the lake's edge when I decided to go for a swim. I've got to get that phone. It has the names of all my friends in the contacts. I can't let her get it.

I turn Cat away from the small spit of sandy beach where the demon Anat shakes with laughter in the moonlight. That closer shore is just a quick trip back into slavery. He fights me, but I win in the end, and he turns where I lead. I only hope he can make it out in time and give me time to shift, get that phone fixed back onto my collar, and shift again before she can get to me.

I could face her down as a man, but I sure don't want to. What a fool to think I'd found a few minutes of peace in that moonlit lake. But no—there's no peace for me, not ever. The minute I find some, there she is, taking it away. Cat is still panicking as his legs pump furiously in the cool water, and I can barely think to plan because I am overwhelmed by his single-minded urge to leave the lake behind.

I'm supposed to be protected. How did she find me?

When Cat hits the shore, he shakes his head and limbs furiously, causing droplets to fling out in all directions. I hear the Cassie-thing bearing down on us and get him moving to where I entered the water. I don't give him time to dry himself. I shift and snatch the phone, clamp it back to my collar, and then shift again after giving it a good tug to make sure it's secure. Two shifts in such a short snip of time is agony. But there's only one choice, and that's to run. Normally a cat would have an advantage in the dark woods, but all bets are off now, because that's no human chasing me.

I can't head for safety at Robert's. That would just endanger the people I care about. I'm truly on my own now. I urge Cat on with every mental prod I can muster into a dense part of the woods where a human-size body will have difficulty following.

Despite this, I hear her crashing through the brush after me. She must be artificially animating Cassie's body now. A human wouldn't have the stamina she shows. But she has to tire soon. Hopefully before she tears up Cassie's body any more on the thorns and branches that must tug at her as she pushes through to follow me.

Cat is tiring and can't keep up the pace much longer. We need to keep an eye out for a place to hide. At the end of these woods, there's a cluster of cabins. I'm certain I know the woods better than Eunice did, even though she'd been renting out the cabins for the fifty years since her first husband died and left them to her.

Behind the third cabin, there's an old drainage pipe. It leads away back toward the lake, depositing runoff from the roofs and gutters of the cabins into it. If I can disappear there, she won't be able to follow unless she's taken up shape-shifting, too.

It's pitch black inside, but Cat has been through this way before. He's a curious explorer, particularly when the scent of prey wafts so temptingly from the tube so often. The ready supply of pooled water makes it a draw for the small, tasty things of the forest.

Cat can no longer move as fast as I'd hoped, and if my tracker knows which way I'm heading, this journey will end in despair. But she can't have me in sight yet because she's still crashing through the undergrowth.

I break out of the woods and race through the yard between two of the cabins and urge Cat to pour on the steam toward the entrance to the drain. He squeezes between the bars that prevent larger animals and children from entering.

Cat's a fighter not a hider, but he hunkers down in the tube as I try to keep him calm and slow his breathing. We sit in total darkness now, ten feet into the drain, well below ground. Cat doesn't like the wet rivulet that runs down the center of the pipe when he sinks to his haunches to rest. He backs up one side of the pipe at an angle.

I hope it works, that I've escaped, but in the dark like this in the narrow drain, I have no way of knowing what's going on outside. I can't shift to make a call, but I won't give into the sense of helplessness that monster pushed into my heart when she called out from the shore.

I wait and I wait and I wait. I'm sure it's been hours. Cat's chilled out now, it's time for a nap. But I'm too tense to give in to it. I have to do something, but if I pop my head out, and she's waiting for me…

What about? I bat at the phone, trying to activate it. It doesn't work at first, but now that Cat has a toy, he persists. It takes forever, but finally, I activate the redial. Robert's voice answers, "Hello? Tom?"

I let Cat get in one good yowl before I force him into silence. I hope that it's enough.

I FOLLOW THE SOUNDS of Tom's feline body traveling through the woods and enhance the girl's vision with a simple spell that allows me to detect his movements more quickly. It isn't hard to follow. He chose a path that wouldn't allow him silence. If he doubles back or veers off, I'll know just by standing completely still for a few moments and listening. I concentrate on the direction he's heading despite the branches that lash and cut.

Human flesh is so limiting, even when pressed on with magical strength. It slows me down.

I need Tom's body for my plans, but I also need to know which witch has undone my magic. None of the witches in Giles should have been able to follow the threads of my spell. They're laughingly weak compared to the sorceresses of my day.

I duck below a branch and raise my arm against another as it rushes toward my face. It wouldn't do to lose an eye or two. When I catch Tom, he'll suffer before his soul disappears forever, and then I'll find and punish his witch as well. How dare anyone undo my handiwork? I'll enjoy watching their pain. Yes, the eyes need to be protected.

Finally. A clearing. I scan it quickly. Nothing moves in front of me. There are no sounds of the chase that I can follow. He must be hiding now, sure he's safe.

I remove the cap from the bottle I'd stowed in a pocket before leaving the shop. I drink and my vision goes black. Not dead. Not the dim reddish-gray canvas of closed eyes. Cat's eyes are open to deep darkness. I have no way to tell where he's gone unless he starts moving in the light again. And I've used the last of the potion. Its effects are already starting to fade, and I haven't got a fresh piece of him to make more.

He's escaped me again. Damn him.

I want to take a chance and pop my head out, but I have no idea how patient this Anat thing is. She could be sitting right outside the entrance to the drain, waiting to ensnare me. I urge Cat back toward the entrance, and he slinks along on his belly because his night vision doesn't work in this kind of blackness. After a few feet, a swath of moonlight appears ahead. We're getting closer to the drain. I prick my ears up, listening for any tell-tale sound from above. There's a leafy scuffling sound. I freeze.

And then my phone rings. That's the end of me if the demon is still out there.

The tiny light dims and the silence is replaced by the sound of Gillian's voice. "All clear, Tom. You can come out now."

I hunch away from the sound. What if it's

Eunice, mimicking Gillian as a lure? I won't follow a siren call.

"Tom? You can come out. It's safe."

I want out of here, and Cat wants away from the wet. But I'm still not sure.

"Tom? Are you afraid it's a trick? I see Cassie's tennis shoe prints all over the place out here in the mud. I recognize that tread. She's worn the same brand since grade school. So we know Anat was here. But it's not a trick. It really is me. Do you remember what you said in London? Do you remember why I followed you here when you wanted me to move to the colonies? You said I was the only one who could save you from yourself. I've never told anyone that. Maybe because I failed so spectacularly. I bet you haven't, either. But I'll always save you if I can. You know I will."

I'm convinced. Gillian would never have told Eunice that. I move through the tunnel as quickly as the darkness allows. When the black gives way to dim slats of gray light, I slip through the bars and look out into early dawn. The first blush of sunrise peeks across the tops of the trees in the east.

A bag comes down over Cat's head, placing me immediately back in darkness. I freeze. I'm caught. I get ready to tear the bag apart with my claws and fight for my life.

Then, Gillian's voice soothes, "Don't freak out, but we need to keep you under wraps until we figure out how Anat found you. So, please don't let

Cat scratch and bite. It's for your own good."

She picks me up and cradles me to her shoulder inside the sack. I recognize Gillian's smell of patchouli and sandalwood. I decide not to tear at the bag right away. She says, "Just sit tight for a little bit longer. Natalie has the motor running."

She calls off toward the cabins, "Robert, I've got him."

I hear another set of footsteps fall in with us as I ride atop her ample bosom, her hand still holding me firmly to her shoulder. Just from the shape of her, I know it really is Gilly. Her softness and warmth is comforting after a night spent tensed for action in the cold and wet.

***

"Find him?" I hear Nat ask after we've trekked a while. "Good."

"Nat has a theory about how Eunice found you, Tom. We know no one could cast a working location spell, so it had to be something else. So, I'm going to set you down, but just stay put for a minute while she checks you out." She sets me down and only the tip of my tail betrays my annoyance with not getting as far away from where I last saw Eunice as possible. It flicks slowly up and down. But no one can see that through the bag.

I hear someone circling around me, breathing heavily. Who knows what Natalie's doing out there.

I envision a tribal dance combined with a series of cheerleader jumps at the finale. She has her red purse with her, of course. In my version of the events, it flings out at odd angles as she gyrates.

When Nat finishes her assessment, which was probably much less fun to watch than what I imagine to amuse myself, she tells the others. "It has the distinct feel of a remote ride-along. Novice stuff. You know, faux warg. She didn't locate him so much as just figure out where he was from what Cat was seeing." The sound of her voice turns to me then. "Tom, I've got something that should prevent her from pulling the same trick again. So, I need to back you out of the bag but keep your head inside for just a while longer."

A tiny slit of daylight appears overhead until a set of hands comes down and lifts me up, backside first, and the bag's drawstring tightens around my neck. Under different circumstances, I'm sure Cat would be having a blast with the opportunity to get himself all tied up in knots getting into and back out of a big cloth bag. But this isn't one of those circumstances. The hands set me down on the dampish grass.

Natalie walks another set of circuits around me and mumbles under her breath while I feel light grains of something hitting my fur.

I catch the scent of herbs and spice. It would make a nice sachet, but I'm not thrilled about wearing it around for any period of time. I smell like my mother's underwear drawer.

Natalie says, "Done," and Gillian pulls the bag off my head. Man, am I glad to see her. Cat winds around her legs, rubbing his head against her in gratitude. When she says, "Let me just throw this blanket over you so you can shift now that that's taken care of," I am more than happy to say my magic words beneath it.

When the shift is over, I scramble up from beneath the blanket, managing to affix it around my waist without flashing everyone.

I look around at them. Natalie is close at hand with her red purse. She's not wearing either a tribal ensemble or a cheerleader sweater, just a fitted pantsuit, her usual attire. Too bad.

Robert leans against the side of his SUV only a few feet away. "If everyone's ready to go?" he says, inclining his head toward the car.

We all pile in.

Once I'm situated alone on the farthest seat in the back, I ask, "How did you find me if you couldn't do a location spell?"

Robert calls back over his shoulder as he starts the car. "That part was easy. I called down to the station and had them ping your cell. There are definite advantages to being mayor. Gave us a good indication of where you'd be. No magic needed."

Gillian adds, "Since we couldn't find you in the open, we started looking for all the hiding places. I almost moved on, but then I got the idea to give you a call even if you couldn't answer."

Yes. That's Gilly. She never gives up on anybody.

***

When we get back to Robert's, he has a message from his Egyptologist friend. "You might as well all be in on this call," he says, as he dials and then puts it on speaker while we settle in together on the comfortable leather sofa and chairs in the study.

"Robert?" comes a voice on the other end of the line. "Those pictures you sent me? Fascinating. I can't stop studying them. Can you arrange for me to see the artifact? I desperately want to see it in person."

"I can ask, Doug. But I don't know if the owner is open to viewings yet. I'll certainly do my best."

"Perfect—yes. They've found a truly unique item. One that, as far as I can tell, until now, was only a rumor with the intact heart and all. Fascinating stories behind this—"

Nat leans forward abruptly and cuts him off. "No need to be a showboat. Tell us what the symbols on the box mean."

There's a pause on the other end of the line. Robert gives Nat a cautioning look and says, "Sorry about that, Doug. The owner is here this morning and asked to sit in silently. You're on speaker."

"Of course, of course. My excitement over the

find is running away with me."

Robert picks up the phone then, giving Nat a pointed look. "My client, while a dear friend, is elderly and can sometimes be abrasive. We can continue without an audience. She's absolutely contrite now. Speaker's off..." He walks to the corner of the large room and leans against one of the dark wood shelves as he talks.

We hear the rest of the conversation one-sided. Way to go, Nat. There are lots of yesses and hmmmms and notes jotted down on the lined yellow paper Robert took with him and balances on a shelf. By the time he's done, I'm ready to tell Doug to get on with it myself.

Finally, Robert presses the off button on the phone after saying, "Thanks, Doug. Yes, it's all invaluable information. I can't thank you enough. I'll see what I can do about that viewing."

He doesn't even have the phone back in the cradle before Nat says, "Well? Details!"

"Nat!" I say. "Give the man time to arrange his thoughts." *But it better not take more than 6.3 seconds.*

Robert raises his eyebrows slightly in acknowledgement. "Doug managed to interpret all of the symbols inside the box, and as we expected, its purpose is as a vessel for Anat's soul. Now, understand that he's fascinated by this as a historian because he has no idea that anything supernatural exists. He views it as mythology, ancient religious practice. I've never told him I'm a warlock. That tends to be a relationship killer the farther you get away from Salem and Giles. His interpretation is going to be colored by academic interest in what he believes is an antiquity. And obviously, he'd really like to get his hands on it for further study."

Nat breaks in. "Who cares about this? Stick to the point. Our time to help that nice young girl that you all seem to care so much about is running out. What does the writing on the box mean?" I have to say I appreciate her impatience on this.

Robert continues, unruffled. "Doug says the heart is a placeholder. The text indicates the box provides a resting place for Anat's soul to prevent her from continuing on to the next world. And as long as her heart remains in the box, it will always call her back from where she is if she becomes disembodied."

"Okay, so why is that such a big thing?" I ask.

"Because we now know that we can destroy the heart once she's out of Cassie and that will end her interference. As to the second box—what we didn't know is that there was a tomb robbery in Egypt recently. The date coincides with when 'Cassie' was out of town. And the only thing that was taken from a tomb full of priceless artifacts was…" Robert pauses, taking a deep breath.

"Oh, for crying out loud, Robert," Nat interjects, "leave out the drama! This isn't a movie of the week."

He responds with his usual patience. "Do you want to hear this, or do you just want to complain?"

"Yes, Nat, just shush, please." Gilly gives her a cautioning look.

"The only thing that was taken, as I was saying before I was interrupted, was the mummy's heart. Just that. The tomb-robber extracted the heart and left everything else alone. The guards who were posted at the entrance to the tomb are still missing. It's all the talk in the archaeological community, but it's not the kind of thing that hits the world news."

"No video surveillance?"

"I asked. Apparently not. The tomb is several hours into the desert. It's isolated. With two armed guards posted at the only entrance, it probably seemed unnecessary."

"And you think this was Eunice or Anat or whoever she is? She went to Egypt to bring back a mummy's heart?" Gillian asks.

"Yes, I believe we should consider it the most likely scenario. Doug says the symbols on the sarcophagus there picture Ba'al with his sisters, Anat and Ashtarte. The face in the large image at the head of the sarcophagus matches exactly with the face of the god Ba'al depicted with his sisters in various erotic and non-erotic poses on the walls of the tomb."

"Well, that's what the second box was made for then, the hot one, the one that burned me when I tried to take it."

"Perhaps. I'd think so, at least. Protecting itself, possibly," Robert agrees.

Gillian turns to me, her voice soft. "Tom, if she's this ready now to go ahead with what she planned…"

"Like hell!" I explode. "This body is not playing host to a parasitic god."

Gillian reaches over and lays a gentle hand on my knee. "Of course not. Not if this circle of witches has anything to say about it. You're right about that."

It's the only time they agree with each other all day, but Natalie and Robert add their voices to the supportive chorus. I'm not so sure any of it will do any good, but by the Goddess, at least I'll go down fighting.

I STILL CAN'T SNIFF OUT a trace of Tom with any of my best locating spells. Damn him!

The crystal globe hits the wall heavily, rattling the paintings on the walls, then falls with a unsatisfying thud to the carpeted floor of the parlor. I expected it to shatter when I flung it away from me. It should have shown me at least a flicker of Tom when I anointed it with the last smear of the ride-along potion I soaked up from the bottom of the bottle. But its interior stayed blank and clear and unhelpful.

Someone must be helping him. He couldn't hide from me by himself. When I find out who's done this thing, that witch will have nowhere to hide. How dare these creatures continue to interfere?

I know he isn't dead. He can't be. He's the perfect vessel, and it would be too ironic if he'd met his end just as his true usefulness to me was coming to be. No, he's alive. Someone has shielded him from me. It has to be Gillian. She had his hair on her couch, after all.

I walk across the room, pick up the globe, and set it on the table. Then I glare at it until it shatters with a satisfying crack. The lumps of fractured crystal fall in a pile onto the tabletop.

"There, that's what happens to those who defy me."

I pick up the phone. It's time for the coven to mobilize and help me out.

***

I move purposefully toward the witches standing in the clearing in the middle of Corey Woods. Some of them look dazed; none of them talk to any of the others. My command gave them one purpose—to wait in the place they'd been called to. To wait for their Goddess to arrive.

"Around me. Make a circle. Quickly."

They scurry like mice until they form a loose circle with me at their center.

"Now sit." I smile to myself. "Sit like the dogs you are and be good."

I turn slowly to look at their blank faces. They'll come to themselves in an hour or so, but until then,

I have a captive audience and enough loaned essence that there's nothing that can stop me from extending my reach and finding Tom, even if he's gone across the country to escape me. It's simply a matter of extracting their energy for my use.

I shuck my pants and jacket, which strips me of all clothing except one of Tom's dashikis. It covers me like a dress, ending halfway down my thighs. I breathe deeply and turn my face to the sky. I can feel the essence of each one of my subjects where they stand. I extend my hands, my fingers spread wide, and the essence flows to me from them. I see the thin, bright, threads the connection makes from the corners of my eyes. I'm the center of a pinwheel made of their immobile bodies.

Their essence empowers me as I reach out, glowing across the trees and further, across the county, seeking the owner of the clothing I wear, comparing the essence of all the creatures I encounter with the tiny flakes of skin left on the dirty clothes from the hamper.

I reach farther and farther still, but there's nothing. Even if he were dead, his body would be detected where it lay. I draw even more power from the witches. I'll suck out their lives entirely if it brings me what I desire. That ancient Winifred is the first to shudder and fall. I let her go. She's given all she can. I don't care.

Zelda falls next, twitching.

I scream to the universe, "WHERE IS HE?".

The universe ignores me.

With a flourish, I release the witches, and the ones who have not yet fallen jerk backward like fish on a broken line. I turn and stalk away with my fingertips still glowing.

I WAKE UP ENERGIZED after Cat's productive hunt the night before. Making french toast with cinnamon and nutmeg as the rest of the household gets moving for the day is a much better use of my time than cowering in a drain pipe. And beating the eggs and cream together is calming. Goddess knows I need some calm.

I've just popped the final piece into the warmer and am setting the table when Robert comes in. The already prominent lines on his forehead and around his eyes are deepened by his tight, worried expression. He carries his cell in his hand. "I just got a call from the Chief of Police, who wondered if an incident last night was 'one of those' he'd want to try to keep quiet. About half of the choir showed up at the hospital, suffering from dehydration, exposure, and exhaustion, as well as being unable to explain much about what happened to them except they'd been in Corey Woods."

His voice breaks and he closes his eyes for a moment. "They had to carry Winnie in. She was in bad shape, unconscious. She didn't make it."

"Sorry, man. Were the two of you close?"

"We grew up together. Winnie, Nat, and I. We all used to play together out in the woods in more innocent times." His voice trails off.

"What are you telling him about the good old days?" Natalie asks as she sashays in, purse dangling from her forearm even at this hour. Gillian follows behind her.

Robert doesn't look like he's up to repeating his story as they take seats at the breakfast table. I fill her in briefly.

"Oh." Natalie's smile fades, then she shakes off whatever she's feeling and says, "No time to be sad, then. It sounds like Anat is on the move, and we can't afford to wait any longer. Anyone think this wasn't her doing? Sucking the life out of people seems to be her MO."

Robert bows his head toward the table momentarily, studying the patterns his liver spots make on the back of his hands.

I say quietly. "You're thinking about Kevin. I'm sorry." His head bobs minutely. "But I agree, Nat. And we can't keep just reacting. She's after me, so let's give me to her. I'll be the bait. We need to get rid of the bitch. I'm tired of doing this the cautious way. Let's find some anti-possession spell, and I'll suggest she meet me somewhere. We have to try."

Gillian says, "No, you can't be bait. We could lose you, too."

"I don't care. We're no closer to rescuing Cassie than we were when we started."

"But I think we are," she replies, holding up a finger to silence me when I start to argue, her other hand moving to Robert's shoulder. "I think that this Anat, whatever she is, has become unstable. Mentally troubled. Last night is just more proof of that. Did you ever see Eunice blow her cool like the Cassie version has done repeatedly?"

Robert raises his head and nods. "You may have something there. It's been years since I've had to call in favors to keep coven activities hushed up, but now? We've had two incidents in which victims have been killed by magical influence within the past two weeks. Not that I think Eunice never had victims. As we got older, I became increasingly sure she did. I just think she cared whether or not they were found and planned her activities accordingly."

"Exactly!" Gillian interjects. "She's suddenly using an extreme amount of magic and leaving a mess in its wake."

I shrug. "Fine. Maybe she's crazy. I don't know. But I'm tired of running. I'm tired of being scared. I'm tired of being without Cassie. I feel like I'm Eunice's prisoner again, and I'm not going to hide any more. She's imprisoned me long enough. So, after we finish breakfast, we're not leaving this table until we have a plan of attack. Goddess help us, we can't wait for the body count to keep rising."

Gillian's fork clatters to the table. "That's it! Do you remember what Aurelie told me? That only a goddess can defeat a goddess? I get it now. That's it! That's the plan!"

***

After Gilly fleshes out her idea, I volunteer for the leading role. No one else should have to risk themselves the way someone is going to have to do. But what I get from her in response is headshaking and naysaying.

"Tom, don't be ridiculous. Of course you can't draw down the Goddess into your body. A goddess is feminine essence. And you, dear one, are as far from feminine as a creature can get." Gillian's head shakes now like one of those bobble-head dolls as she emphasizes her point.

Nat snorts, and I feel her eyes traveling over me inch by inch. "I'll second that, dear."

Gilly rolls her eyes at Nat then turns back to me. "It's just that it has to work exactly as we plan it, and I'm the only possible candidate. Nat has been openly denying the existence of the Goddess for years, so the Goddess isn't going to be receptive to her. I, on the other hand—I've been loyal. I always knew she was out there, lending me a hand when I truly needed and deserved it."

"But you're going to be asking a Goddess, the same thing that Anat claims to be, to take over your body." I hold the book with the slavering demon-goddess woodcut Robert had collected from the library toward her over the table. I shove the image of the contorted creature with breasts and horns and fur and long, sharp teeth right up in her face. "That's what you're inviting in."

"Don't be ridiculous, Tom. I've participated in dozens of drawing ceremonies in my lifetime, and in each of them, I could feel the essence of the goddess within me. Her power was warm, loving, and motherly. She wouldn't hurt me. If she could take me against my will, why hasn't she ever taken me before now? No, it's settled. The new moon is in two days. We'll do the drawing ceremony then. Natalie and I have the plan nailed down, and with the goddess's help, I'm sure we'll succeed."

I turn to Robert, who has been silent for all of the arguments over the past hour. "What about you?"

"After what she did to Kevin and Winifred? The plan may not be my style, and I certainly worry about putting Gillian at risk, but this time, I'm all in."

CAT BATS AT A HAIR TIE he finds floating around in the bottom of Gillian's gigantic hippie purse. He's happier now about the bumpy ride on her hip with something to occupy him. I can't say I'm thrilled with the travel arrangements, but until there's something going on out there that I need to pay attention to, a hair tie gets my focus. I mean, what adult male wants to deal with the fact that for huge periods of his life, people can stick him in a purse and carry him around like a snotty hanky? I could murder myself a hair tie right about now.

It fights back about as well as a non-living object can do by getting stuck on a claw and stretching, then snapping when it lets go. It's fun, if I don't think about it too much. If I could just stretch it out a little longer without it springing

241

back…

Wait, she's talking. My ears perk up. Time to make this humiliating handbag experience worthwhile.

"It's been so long since I've seen you, Maureen. I thought I'd stop by and find out how you're getting along." She reaches into the bag and grabs onto and lifts out a bottle of red wine that's been sharing my space as she continues. "Anything to report on the grandmother front? I've got just the right thing to celebrate, if so, or to commiserate if the news isn't good."

"Yes, come on in. Oh, do I have something to celebrate!" I peek out over the top of the bag as Maureen leads us to an overstuffed couch and then continues on through the dining room where she stops at a dark wood sideboard. "I'll just get us some glasses, shall I?"

When she returns with two glasses and a corkscrew, I pull my head back in and listen to the sound of the cork being yanked from the bottle. It sounds like it comes out easily, although it was a much more difficult job the first time Gillian uncorked it. But Maureen would have no idea about the extra ingredient. Apparently, she can pour the stuff down but can't tell the difference between Dom Perignon and Ripple. Maureen continues on happily about her daughter's impending motherhood. I sneak my head up and risk a peek out again.

"Triplets! Do you believe it? Must have happened months ago. Although I'm surprised she didn't mention it." Her happy mask slips off for just a second, and a worried face shows beneath. Then her smile returns. "It's so exciting!"

As I duck back down into the depths of Gilly's purse, I'm surprised it's not an entire litter. Too much of a coincidence for me. And the way Maureen's face changed for just that moment? She knows it, too.

Maureen's happiness as she discusses her grandchildren-to-be fades over the next ten minutes. As her words slur more and more, she yawns, moving her hand to her mouth languidly and then apologizes. "How rude of me. I can't imagine why I'm so tired. It must be the excitement. I've been ecstatic since she told me yesterday evening. It's obviously wearing me to a frazzle."

Gillian stands up, and I swing wildly back and forth for a moment in the bag. "That's all right, dear. I need to be getting on anyway. Have another glass of wine. Relax." Gillian leans in to her as she passes and gives her a quick hug around the shoulders. "You're going to be a grandmother— you've earned it."

Gillian closes the door behind her to the sounds of Maureen's snores.

"You know, Tom, I feel wrong about that." But

I can hear the smirk in her voice. She hustles down the street to meet up with Nat.

***

I stick my head out for the breeze while Gillian walks to the end of the street where Natalie sits in the driver's seat of her old Dodge, music turned on loud to an oldies station. She bops along to the beat and turns with a huge grin when Gillian pulls open the driver's side door and slides in, nearly knocking me back into the bottom of the purse as she readjusts. I scramble out as quickly as possible and head to the back seat.

"That was fun, wasn't it? I haven't had this much fun in years!" Nat throws her head back, practicing a witchy cackle. "We should have a demon infestation more often."

Gillian laughs with her. "Yes, it was. Despite a little guilt, it was fun. Maureen's eyes locked on that bottle of red the second I pulled it out of my bag. If I'd gone there to poison her, she'd be turning blue right now instead of snoring to wake the dead." She wipes away a happy tear with the back of her hand.

"Oh no, it couldn't have been easier than Zelda and chocolate. I thought she'd gnaw my arm off trying to get to them! We certainly do know our neighbors, don't we? I suppose we'll have to draw straws for Dora?"

"No, I say together. Why should only one of us

have all the fun?"

Natalie pulls the Dodge into Dora's driveway. Gilly offers me the open mouth of her purse, but I flick my tail and give her slitty eyes from my comfortable spot on the backseat. There's nothing I'm going to learn at Dora's. Maybe if I was a were-poodle, I'd get into riding around in someone's purse, but nah. It's not for this cat. Way too confining. I'll sit this one out.

Fifteen minutes later, they hurry out, arm in arm, giggling like schoolgirls, and jump back into their respective seats.

Gilly tells her co-conspirator, "This would be awful if we actually meant to harm them, but since it's for a good cause, I guess it's okay to enjoy it. But, oh, I'd feel bad if this wasn't to keep them out of Anat's reach tonight."

Nat pulls the rearview her direction and touches up her bright red lipstick before putting it back. "You're such a goody two shoes. Lighten up. We'll be dead soon enough. Plenty of time to be boring then. Besides, you know as well as I do that this will protect them as much as it helps us—don't forget what Anat did to them the last time she enthralled them." She starts the car up and looks behind before she pulls out.

"Do you think we should have propped her up before she fell into the cupcakes? All that frosting is going to make quite a mess."

"Yes it is, dear!" Natalie howls with laughter

again. It's infectious. Gillian joins her. They both laugh so hard and long that I'm afraid Natalie will land us in a ditch rather than get us back to headquarters.

When Robert opens the door to his back patio to let us in, his brow wrinkles as they both burst out laughing at his serious expression. "What's wrong with you? Did you get into the wine before you doctored it?"

"No, Robert, we're just tired of acting our age and decided to take a vacation from being fuddy-duddies. You should try it some time." Natalie gives him a slap on the backside as she passes by.

If I had a feather on me, I'd lob it at him to see if it knocks him over. But I don't have a feather, so I pad silently around him, figuring the cat's got his tongue right now every bit as much as it has mine.

***

Robert sets the contents of his brown bags out on the table top in a row for the other witches to inspect.

"I managed to get everything you asked for. I have to say, the shops in Salem don't carry the stock like they used to. Mostly ticky-tacky for the tourists these days. We've lucked out with Eunice running things here for so long. I had to visit four different places before I was able to pick up everything we need, and I wasn't sure I was going to find the asafetida powder." He hands a plastic bag to Gillian, who opens it and gives it a sniff.

"Goodness yes, that's nasty. Just the thing."

"Fortunately I asked, and one of the—what do they call them—gosh girls? The ones who wear black and want to date vampires? She said they had some they were saving for a regular customer, but she couldn't possibly let me have it. I managed to talk her out of the lot of it at a pretty price." Robert scowls when he hints at the overpayment. He may be wealthy, but I bet it doesn't sit well with his East Coast parsimony.

I buck up for what's coming next. "Well, I'm ready, then. Time to get into place, make me visible, and let the old mummy get me on her radar."

Gillian's face sobers. "You don't have to. We can figure something else out."

"Gillian, I admit it, I've never been more scared of anything, but that fear isn't going to make me run away from what I need to do this time." It feels very human to say that in front of these people who have earned my trust. They're not going to use it against me. Not even Nat. "The very thought of being caught and used again by that thing, whatever it is, terrifies me. But all I've wanted for over forty years is another chance to be a real man. And I'm not even close if I can't give everything I've got to save the girl who gave a home to my lost soul."

Gillian leans forward and pats my hand, giving

me a sad smile. She doesn't say so, but she knows as well as I do that it's possible some of us might not survive this. I squeeze her hand tight. I want to say something more, but there aren't words for how I feel about her, about these people, my friends, right now.

Natalie turns away from the private moment, digging through the bags. "Robert, are there no bones? I need something light—a sparrow or some other smallish bird," she says when the silence continues too long.

"I've got a couple of cuts of meat we can get some segments of bone out of if you want to dig into our dinners for the week, but no bird." Robert walks to the big fridge and surveys its contents, shaking his head to confirm. "I'm not a poultry fan."

"Well, how does anyone expect me to accentuate Gillian's drawing spell if I haven't got anything in the mix to allow her spirit to soar toward the goddess as they come together?" Natalie huffs and puts her hands on her hips.

I stand up. Cat's fantasizing about running down one of those big, white turkeys at a farm on the edge of town to help her out, but I've got a more realistic idea he can put into action immediately. "Geez, Nat. Give a guy a chance before you get all bent out of shape."

***

I shift inconspicuously behind some bushes in Robert's immense back garden. Within minutes, Cat skims across the lawn, heading for the bushes in the back where the birds fight over the wild berries along the fence line.

I sink low on my haunches, my belly skimming just above the evenly trimmed grass and move forward one nearly imperceptible step at a time, my eyes never leaving my prey. When I spring, I catch a sparrow as it takes flight and trap it beneath a paw. Cat's neat teeth sink into its neck as the bird's luckier buddies escape.

I stop Cat from ripping the bird apart so he doesn't scatter the bones. He's not used to me refusing him his spoils, but I have to get the bird back to the house relatively intact.

I'm back into my jeans, shirt untucked, when I drop the carcass onto the counter. "Sparrows I can do. Anything bigger, and you can stop by the butcher's."

She snorts dismissively. "It's about time you contributed." She grabs a knife from a wooden storage block and hands it to me. "Debone that dear. And try to keep the bones as intact as possible if you could."

Nat's all business now, despite the dig about my contribution to the magical side of things.

It's time for us all to focus. No more

daydreaming about turkey hunts or quibbling about bones.

We're going to war.

"YOU ARE NOT making me drink that," I protest.

Natalie uses a small kitchen strainer to dip out large chunks from the pot of vile-smelling sludge she's cooked up for me from some of the ingredients Robert bought. She's also mixed in a small glass of my own reluctantly supplied urine.

"It's disgusting, isn't it?" She grins. "We could try applying it to your skin like the last one. Probably wouldn't be effective, but it would be fun. Go ahead and strip down while I get into the right frame of mind." Her grin spreads even broader. So much for the all-business attitude when she's working with magic.

Gillian steps in, her voice raised a notch. "Nat, stop taunting him. How much of that does he have to drink?" How did my ex-wife end up being my mother?

"No need to get testy, dear. All in good fun. A little gallows humor, as they say. He doesn't need to drink much, and I still need to strain it before it's ready."

I put a hand on Gillian's shoulder. I know her. When she starts to snip, she's stressed. "You okay?"

"I'm just...I'm scared."

"We all are, I think." I massage her neck gently, working at the tense muscle there.

"But you could lose your freedom again."

"And you could end up possessed by a demon-goddess, despite your protestations that *the* Goddess is a good goddess and will protect you. So, neither one of us is looking at a rosy outcome if it all goes south."

She flashes me a half smile. "Suddenly, I'm feeling the kind of tired you get when your body decides to announce you're old and there's no going back. That kind of tired." She reaches up to pat my hand where I'm still kneading her shoulder.

I catch her hand and give a squeeze and lean in to plant a friendly kiss on her cheek. It perks her up, you can tell.

"Great wallowing warthogs, Gillian, do you have to suck up every bit of male attention in a room?" Natalie barks.

Gillian gives her a look I can't quite interpret as Natalie hands me a small jar that I slide into a pouch and affix to my collar.

I'd asked if I could meet them in the woods. I want to give Cat one last night on the prowl, just in case one or both of us doesn't make it. Then again, he's got two lives left, and I've only got the one: maybe he should be giving me a big last night out. I shift, and I'm out the door to bound over Robert's back fence, moving toward Corey Woods. It needs to be there, in the place of the Giles witches' power, that Anat discovers me. I hope we pull it off. If not...

I bat the thought away and focus instead on the musky smells to each side as I lope along. My ears swivel to each small sound that signals the movement of a mouse or mole through the rotted leaves below the trees.

As much as Cat is a predator, even he is aware he is also prey. There's always something bigger and stronger out there waiting to pounce. But a cat doesn't think deeply: he would never be aware of death stalking behind his left shoulder. As the poet once said, it's only man who has an angel's brain and sees the axe from the first.

Maybe I wouldn't mind so much if it was an axe: an axe is swift. But if it's a tether again...no, I can't think of that. And I can't think of Cassie jailed inside her body with no control of what it does, subject to the whims of the mad being who stole her life.

As much as I can't bear the thought of being put on a leash again, I'd sooner do it than leave Cassie trapped.

I kick it into higher gear. No distractions. One goal.

I'm going to put that demon down.

*****

With Cat's night-vision superpower, I watch Robert, Natalie, and Gillian pick their way carefully through the woods on the old path. It hasn't been used by anyone except for a few hikers for years, and it's overgrown. There are places where it's nearly completely obscured by brush and a fallen tree or two. Another three members of the coven follow them. They're the only ones left who Anat has never enthralled. The rest should be sleeping soundly from the draughts they took either willingly or unwillingly. Nothing can be left to chance. Anat needs to be on her own for this one, and my merry band needs to have all their ducks in a row. I watch from a safe distance, ready to bolt and draw the demon away if she shows up too early.

The old stone altar is still in place. Rumors say the coven abandoned it in the twenties after an unfortunate incident in which a local warlock took things too far and sacrificed his second wife there in hopes of bringing back his first one. It was a spell that was unlikely to succeed as his first wife had been dead for several years. It did, however, result in the original coven grounds being tainted by bad zombie juju, and no one really wanted to return. But the ground is still consecrated to the goddess, and we need that. We also need a place Anat wouldn't think to look for us, and this one fills that bill.

Natalie removes the ribbon tie from around the cloth-wrapped object she carries and unrolls the cloth to reveal the ritual athame, and a wand with a phallus-shaped head. When Robert first whipped it out for the others to view at the house, Natalie chuckled a little too loudly for everyone's comfort. But Robert shut her down with a particularly high-priestly glare, telling her it was a sacred object, one not to be laughed at. He needs the special magic of the wand during the ritual if Gillian is to successfully draw the goddess down for a full possession of her body.

Eunice had ended the annual drawing ceremony when she became high priestess. She always insisted that the Goddess invested her at all times, which left no reason to draw her down on special occasions. In the current context, her assertion takes on new meaning. Yes, she was invested. Or more accurately, infested, with a goddess—just not Gillian's good and helpful one.

When we were planning, Gillian said she'd participated in the drawing ceremony a few times before Eunice brought it to an end. Robert and Natalie had been observers, but as atheists, they had never taken active roles. Gillian could make no promises about what would happen, but in the previous rituals, she had no doubt that the Goddess had passed through her. But those ceremonies had been communal events in which the participants had all been a little fried from earlier passing around a pipe full of non-magical herb. It was the sixties—even witches keep up with the times. Some later denied anything had happened. But Gillian believes it had. Saving Cassie absolutely depends on her belief.

The witches don their robes and stand quietly, waiting.

Natalie places the tools she needs on the altar so that they'll be enclosed in the casting of the circle. There are four candles—green, red, yellow, and blue to represent earth, fire, air, and water. She also places a bowl of water and a bowl of salt. Then she picks up the athame and begins.

Gillian, Robert, and the other coveners stand a short way off from the circle. She turns to them and says, "Let it be known that the circle is about to be cast. All who enter must do so in perfect love and perfect trust."

She checks a compass quickly to make sure that she knows which direction is north and leaves a door open there, then she solemnly makes her first circle with the athame. Having finished, she makes the second and third circles in the same manner.

After completing the circles, she lights the candles and places them in the four quarters. As an eclectic with loyalty to the universe, not to the Goddess, Natalie's invocation as she lights each of the candles is brief. At each corner, it is merely, "Watch over those who enter here in perfect love and perfect trust."

I shift to human form and throw down the vile potion I'd stowed in my pouch and then cast the bottle aside. It tastes nowhere near as bad as it smells, which is only a small blessing. Leaning naked against a tree in the dark, the rough bark biting into my skin, and watching the ring in the dim light of the candles, I'm chilled, I'm hyper alert, and I'm counting down in my head how long I have before Anat comes racing to Corey Woods to find me. If I'm right, she'll sense me immediately. But there's no point leaving it to chance.

I grab the phone off my collar and make a call. I call her on the shop phone number so that caller ID will show my name. When she answers, I say. "Got a fix on me, lover? I'm in Corey Woods. Come and get me." I tap the button to end the call. It isn't the chill night that makes me shiver.

From within the circle the High Priestess announces, "The circle is cast. You may enter."

Robert walks to the invisible door first. Natalie stands blocking his path. "How do you enter the circle?"

He replies, "In perfect love and perfect trust."

Natalie stands aside and Robert walks past her. Gillian is next. Her response is the same. The other three witches follow.

Once they're all inside, Natalie draws a pentacle with the athame to close each of the concentric circles. It's complete. They are as safe as they can be with ancient supernatural beings hanging around town and can now leave the circle safely only by cutting it with the sacred blade, the athame.

Gillian moves to stand facing the altar, her hands crossed over her chest. As High Priest, Robert kneels in front of her and uses the wand to trace the shape of the pentacle in the air between them.

"I invoke and beseech thee, O mighty Mother of all life and fertility. By seed and not, by stem and bud, by leaf and flower and fruit, by life and love, do I invoke thee, to descend into the body of thy servant, Gillian."

He leans into Gillian then, bending to plant a kiss lightly on the top of her foot. "Blessed be thy feet, that have brought thee in these ways."

He kisses her knees, then her belly to represent her womb, her breast, and her lips, speaking the blessing in turn for each of them.

After each blessing, the other witches quietly intone, "Blessed be."

Robert stands then and moves back a little, although he's impeded by the altar behind him. He bows his head to Gillian and asks, "Goddess, are you with your servant?" He looks up, and he backs away abruptly to smack hard against the altar stone when he sees the expression on Gillian's face. It's rage. Pure, undistilled rage. That emotion can't be Gillian's.

It's time for me to go. Anat will have had enough time to jump into a car and get most of the way here. There's only a few minutes left before she arrives. All I can do is hope that the rage on Gillian's face is directed at Anat instead of the others.

As I run toward the parking lot closest to the ritual grounds, Gillian's voice rings out loudly behind me.

"Stay here," she tells the witches. "You are not safe outside this circle tonight. Priestess, I need the knife."

I turn back to look. I shouldn't, I need to head off Anat and keep her away from the ritual grounds where they'll wait, but it's only a moment to make sure they're safe.

If Natalie's trust isn't perfect, everything we've planned will be undone. She doesn't flinch. She hands the knife to the woman who looks like Gillian but no longer sounds or moves like her. This woman is commanding, strong. Gillian's strength comes from her softness, not from authority. This isn't Gillian faking it. The Goddess has been drawn down.

I take off for the parking lot to meet Anat, hoping Gillian and the Goddess inside her are close behind me. I can't wait any longer to have my

Cassie back. Whatever the Goddess plans to do with that knife, the witches who called her are on their own.

I WRAP CAT'S TAIL neatly around his body, holding our head erect. He's ready to unsheath his claws at a moment's notice. I watch the gravel parking lot where I expect the Cassie-thing to appear, the tip of my tail twitching swiftly up and down in big, twisting arcs. I can't think of her as a goddess. I won't. Goddess means something so much different to me than what Cassie has become.

I know I can't take her down on my own, but I had to be the lure. This had to happen where the witches are strong and the risk of bystanders getting hurt is low. What else could draw her here unprepared?

The econo-car barrels into the lot at its magically induced top speed of 55. The brakes squeal, and it slides for a few feet, accompanied by the crunching sound of gravel beneath the wheels. When the Cassie-thing steps out of the driver's side, I hold my ground. Cat's hackles rise involuntarily, causing the fur on his back to make a stiff peak across his spine. I will win or lose today. Either way, I'll have stood my ground and faced down my fate like a man despite my feline features.

She runs toward me, binding me before she even reaches me, with a wave of her hands and a flash of light. A small test of my range of motion confirms that I can move my limbs, but I can't leave this spot.

"So, you decided to come back to me? Good Tom." That sounds nowhere near as friendly as you might expect.

I'd anticipated the transformation: there are no surprises when it starts. I know better than to fight it—that will only increase the pain. My bones crack, stretch, elongate. My skin pulls taut and my jaw and head push outward, fur turning to hair to bare skin. She'll want to see my expression when she does whatever she's going to do to me.

When I'm a man again, I retest my magical bond and I'm still stuck to the spot. I dart a glance toward the woods, hoping to see Gillian bringing her passenger along as reinforcements, but there's no one there.

"Who are you, really?" I demand, stalling her, even though I know the answer. "You're not Cassie, and I don't think you're even Eunice."

She throws her head back and laughs like a silent movie villain. She'll twirl her moustache and tie me to the railroad tracks in the next scene, I bet. "My true name is Anat. I suppose it's time that we were properly introduced, given our intimate history. I'm a goddess, Tom—what better being for you to serve all those years then me? And soon, your delicious body will serve a god. Your spirit, of course, will have to be suppressed for that. Too bad. So sad. I'll miss our time together." She walks a circle around me as she talks and leans into my ear from behind for her last words. "But I'll let Ba'al know about the things you did that I liked." Her tone is meant to be seductive, I'm sure. But to me, it just sounds needy and pathetic.

"Some goddess. You have to enslave a man to keep a lover. And when you can't keep that one, you have to drag one out of his tomb."

She places a hand on each of my shoulders. Her nails dig into the bare skin. "You were never my lover. You were just a toy."

"I don't think so. I think you were lonely. I think no one loves you. I think no one ever has."

Pressure slams down on me from her palms, pushing me toward the ground until I lay flat, my lungs compressed between the ground and the force. I gasp for air, but she's crushing the breath out of me. If she keeps it up, there'll be nothing left of me to use. I'd take that over being her lover's surrogate, but not before I free Cassie.

I keep fighting my invisible bonds with the strength I take from Cassie's face smiling at me in the eyes of my heart.

My vision goes spotty.

And then—that's Gillian's voice I hear behind me. The voice of the woman I'd loved and wronged, but with something new hidden in those familiar tones. Something frightening.

"Release him, Anat. You've played with him long enough. He isn't yours anymore."

Anat's head snaps around to look at her challenger. She laughs, but the pressure holding me down recedes and I sit up again, gasping, turning toward the sound of that welcome voice.

Anat runs toward her full tilt, her head down like a battering ram.

Gillian disappears and reappears behind her, to stand in front of me, shielding me. "No, Anat. This one will leave with me. You have no right to him."

She reaches into the folds of her robe and removes the box we'd hidden beneath the art gallery. She opens the lid.

"Don't you see: I have something you want. I'll trade you—your Ab Khr for this man's soul. Or are you willing to lose yours to keep his?"

An image of Anat's true self begins to form as an outline around Cassie, more and more solid in appearance as the seconds tick past. Her true eyes, transparent but open in front of Cassie's, narrow to slits. "Where? How did you get it?" Anat's voice goes up the scale, ringing with alarm.

"It was easy to steal. You are simple. Predictable." She walks to the side, drawing Anat's attention away from me. She reads the words on the back of the box. Anat's shadow form is pulled toward Gillian and away from Cassie. Anat pulls back against the power that tugs her like a dog on a leash, but the pull is too strong.

"I don't want to inhabit you, you crone!" Anat rages as she's drawn toward Gillian, fighting it all the way.

I transform myself while she's distracted, making myself as small a target as possible, and when I'm done, the hairs in Cat's coat rise with the blowback of the magical charge. I test my ability to move from the spot where I'm stuck and find the spell has dissipated now that Anat is occupied by her own troubles.

As Anat's essence is drawn away, Cassie's body drops to the ground. I can tell there are still pieces of Anat's essence sticking to it—the aura it projects is red and angry. Then, the trailing wisps of energy let go when she's near enough Gillian's body to enter.

But Gillian is already possessed. Anat's entry is blocked.

Her apparition flares, howling. Anat has nowhere to go.

I can't stand here and watch when I need to act. I run to Cassie and butt her with the top of my head. She's unresponsive. I put Cat's sensitive nose near hers, and her breath warms it. Still alive.

I want to shift and carry her out of here, but I worry it will draw Anat's attention our way. I don't know if she can force her way back into a body once she's out, and I don't want to find out. Cat sits sentinel, ready for Anat if she comes.

On the battlefield, only twenty feet away, the Goddess matches Anat, making her true form visible now. "There are those who give their bodies willingly to a goddess when that goddess will treat it with respect and return it unharmed. But you don't know that, do you? You're no goddess at all, you have no ability to bring enlightenment or goodness to those who are loyal to you. No, as Ba'al always said of us—Astarte is the goddess, but Anat is a demon. Why do you think he allowed himself to be freed to the universe after I made that choice myself? And why do you think he imprisoned your chosen maiden so she could not come to you—did you never question why she did not return so that you could be reborn?"

Anat's apparition is fading now, no longer hanging together in a semi-solid shape. Wispy trails of it disperse into the air. "Liar! Ba'al always preferred me over you! Always!"

The essence that surrounds and protects Gillian grows, towering over her. The demon grows in height to match her, increasingly transparent the more she extends herself.

"It's time to let go, Anat. I love you, despite your flaws. You are my sister. Come join me."

"No!" She screams and turns, heading for Cassie again. As Cat, I move just as swiftly, leaping to her, tearing with both claws, and a slice of the demon's essence shreds beneath them. Anat reaches out with one filmy hand and casually snaps his neck.

Cat dies without pain after the quick dispatch of his nervous system, his disconnected brain first flaring to bright light then dimming as life leaves him. *How many lives left? One. He still has one. I'll be safe…I'm sure I'm safe.*

Blackness. Then my living human body unfolds from his dead one. I am there for only a moment when the shift begins again, pulling me back to the final life of the living Cat.

When Cat comes back, Anat is standing over Cassie, digging her hands in at her chest, slowly making progress pushing her essence back in.

"Anat!" her sister calls. "Move away from her. You can't take a human who's unwilling. You know that. She hasn't read your words this time. I *will* destroy the Ab Khr."

Anat removes her hands and turns, then laughs. "And yet you're not holding it anymore, are you, sister?"

And she's right, the box is at Gillian's feet. When did she set it down? What went on when I was gone?

Anat holds out her hands, and a silver tendril

snakes out as another wraps itself swiftly around Gillian's arms, keeping her from reaching out to keep the box safe.

No way, not the old tractor beam trick. I leap as a tiny but confident panther, saying my shift words as I go, and land as Tom. I beat the beam by seconds. I open the box, snatch the heart, and fling the box away. As it flies, I tear at the dried out clump of nasty goddess gristle with both hands. It deteriorates quickly as I rip and rend.

Anat howls as she fades to a mass of smoke, her keening turning into the sound of the wind. At the side of the clearing, a dog howls in sympathy.

The smoke-thing swirls, orienting itself toward the edge of the clearing, where the large, black dog stands, muzzle in the air. It whooshes toward the howl, dead leaves swirling after. I brush my hands together rapidly. The powdery remnants of the heart that allowed her to move from body to body are picked up by the wind and dispersed.

If she made it to that dog, she better be stuck there.

***

The Goddess goes when the demon does. Gillian slumps to the ground, then sits up, looking shaken, but she appears to be okay other than that. I cradle the still unconscious Cassie as I call to her. "I can't go after her. I'm sorry. I can't leave Cass."

"She's not hurting us now. No reason to follow her."

I press my lips to Cassie's forehead and smooth her hair with one hand, willing her to come all the way back to me.

I address Gilly but I don't take my eyes off Cassie's face. "Is the Goddess…"

"Yes, she's gone. She doesn't like to directly interfere, but she's been watching Anat for a long time…"

Gillian stands up and takes off her black robe, handing it to me. She wears a flowing white cotton dress beneath. "Cover yourself, and let's see about our girl."

I put the robe on, and it barely covers my knees.

Gillian holds Cassie's wrist for a moment. "Strong pulse. That's a good sign." She pulls the athame from behind her back where it had been shoved into her belt. "I hate to ask it, but you do need to leave her now. Take this to the others. Cut the circle so they can exit safely and not set loose any more negative magic today. Nat needs to take a look at Cass as soon as possible so we can get her to the house or the hospital, one of the two. I'd do it myself so you could stay, but the Goddess asked something of me before she left. I think we owe her, don't you?"

I take the knife reluctantly, press my forehead

against Cassie's as a promise, and I'm on my way. I don't want to leave her like this, but Natalie can help her more than I can now.

I come back from the twilight: I no longer feel the pressure of that other soul thrusting me into the farthest corner of my own body. Did they put Anat to sleep again? Where's Tom? I try to sit up, but I'm too weak to move much of anything. My body feels heavy, weighed down.

Then I see Gillian through a field of dark, shifting spots. She reaches her hand out tentatively to touch the lid of a box. Omigod! No! I want to yell, stop her from being taken.

She opens the lid. Through the spots, I see the shuddering lump inside it. No way. Disembodied hearts don't beat. She raises it over her head, looking up to the sky and holding it at the end of her outstretched arms, speaking quietly. "Thank you, Goddess, for your strength. I will always come to you in perfect love and perfect trust." At least my ears are working okay even though my eyes are wonky.

She continues talking, something about release and freedom from earthly bonds. Then, sparks leap from the heart into the night, twisting and breaking into smaller particles until they disperse and she's holding just a dried lump of gristle. She pulls one hand into a fist around it. When she opens her hand to the breeze, the particles blow away.

Whatever that was? Ick.

I'm starting to feel in control of myself again. There's not a trace of that evil nutjob in here. I try my voice.

"Gillian?" It's weak and unsure, but it's totally my voice again, not someone else's.

Gillian wipes her hands on her dress, leaving long dirty trails, before she scrambles to me across the grass and pulls me into a giant hug. "Oh Goddess, I wish I hadn't sent Tom to get the others. He should be here."

"What was that? What you did?"

"Tying up loose ends, sweetheart. Putting a god back where he belongs. I think it's clear that gods and goddesses should never inhabit the same world with mortals."

She folds me into her arms for a long time.

I RUSH ALONG as fast as I can go in a long robe with bare feet. I need to start planning my wardrobe better. Maybe I could tuck a pair of jockey shorts around my collar in preparation for an unanticipated need to shift. Shoes would still be a problem, though. And underpants hanging from a cat's neck? No, nobody will think that's strange, I'm sure.

I'm at the old ritual grounds within minutes.

"Where's north?" I ask.

"Natalie points in a line from the altar to a tree.

I sight on the tree and walk in toward the circle until Nat says, "There. The outside radius."

I cut the first circle with the athame, then walk in two paces and cut the next, then another two steps to cut the third.

"So, what just ran past here? Big dog, red eyes? Stopped and growled? I think it was trying to bully us into leaving the circle." Natalie holds out her hand for the knife.

I hand it to her as I reply. "Glowing red eyes?"

"I'd definitely say they were glowing," Robert answers.

Oh hell. It can't just be over. Of course not. "I'm not sure. It could be Anat. I mean, obviously, it's Anat. But we got her out of Cassie, and I destroyed the heart. The plan worked."

Nat motions with her head to the crystal ball sitting on the altar. "We saw a lot of it in there, courtesy of the Goddess. Must have missed the part where you unleashed a doggy-demon on Giles."

"We'll deal with it when we deal with it. But both Cassie and Gillian are safe."

Robert claps me on the back. "Good to hear. Yes, very, very good to hear."

I relax when I realize it really is over. "I don't know how to repay all of you," I say, as I look around at the small group of witches.

"Give us a striptease at my next birthday celebration, and we'll call it even," Nat says, grinning. The other lady witches titter.

"If that's what it takes, Nat, you got it."

I'm impatient to get back to Cassie, but the oldsters can't move at my pace. I think about ditching them to dash back to be with her, but after all they've done for me, leaving them in the middle of the woods with what might be a possessed demon dog doesn't sit right with me. The conscience I've gotten back since I started spending more time as a man than as a cat can be a real bear. I hold myself back, but inside I'm hyped to break into a run to be with Cassie.

It feels like forever before I get a glimpse through the thinning trees of Cassie sitting up in the grass with Gillian, Gillian's arms wrapped around her, her head on Gillian's shoulder.

I can't hold back any longer. The trailing witches will still be within shouting distance if I take off. I break into a run, ignoring the sticks and stones that tear at my bare feet. I'll worry about them later. That's my girl over there. She's back. It's time to take her home.

Cassie must have heard me pounding toward her. Her head lifts from Gillian's comforting shoulder, swiveling toward me, an expression of alarm on her face. She laughs and cries all at once when she sees it's only me.

She stands to come to meet me, and I catch her just as her knees give out beneath her. I support her with my enfolding hug as our lips meet and the world goes away around us. She smells of Eunice's perfume, but I know the gentle touch of her mouth on mine. Eunice had no concept of gentle. This is my loving Cassie.

Reluctantly, I leave her lips to whisper in her ear, "I love you. Goddess knows, I love you."

Then we're both crying and laughing, and we suddenly remember we have an audience when Robert clears his throat. "It's awkward breaking this up, but we need to head home. Hell of a night." He shakes his head and turns away, repeating, "Hell of a night."

***

"You don't have to carry me. I'm still weak, but I can walk," Cassie says with a yawn.

I kiss her on the top of the head as blue sparks

leap from Gillian's fingers to unlock the front door of the shop. "Do you really think I would let go of you right now?"

Gillian says, "Night, you two," then walks back to Robert's waiting SUV. I nod to her, and then flash an eyebrow-lift, chin-thrust goodbye to Robert and Natalie. I get nods back. Cassie's head crashes against my shoulder. She's only semi-conscious now.

There's no way I'm sleeping tonight. I'll just stay up and watch her breathe.

***

Three days after I carried Cassie up to our bed, I lean across the counter to plant a kiss on the tip of the world's cutest nose. "Swept, stocked, and ready to open, Miss Proprietor."

Cassie giggles. "That's Ms. Proprietor to you, Mr. I-Need-To-Get-With-The-Times. So, get that door unlocked, minion. Don't just stand around wasting time kissing people's noses."

I unlock and prop the door to let the perfect summer day find its way inside. It isn't long before Natalie bustles in. Right on time to pick up her facial treatment. We lean into each other for a hug, and Cassie beams at her.

"One Magic Youth Masque coming up, Nat." She reaches under the counter where the day's stock of perishable items is stored in the small fridge, then sets the jar of cream on the counter.

"You know, Nat, before you go with that...well, Tom and I have discussed this..." She looks to me, and I realize she's going to tell Natalie what's in the masque. I look around, trying to figure out the safest place to duck out of the way. "Well, some of the ingredients in your masque are kind of...kind of..."

"Ground fetal pig, that kind of thing, you mean?" She waves her hand, dismissive. "I analyzed the very first batch and sorted that out years ago. But you see my skin, don't you? Smooth as a fetal pig's behind. If I could make it myself, I would. But the magic Eunice added, that's something else entirely. I've tried, but I can't replicate it. It's just not one I have a talent for. I am more than glad that you do."

"Oh. In that case, no problem. Same time next week?"

"Of course, dear." She picks up her bag and says, "And the two of you, you're still coming to our little adventurer's club at Robert's tonight?"

"Wouldn't miss it for the world," I reply. "Gillian would hex the both of us. And anyway, I'm doing the cooking."

"Excellent. See you there. And Tom, my birthday's coming up next month. I expect you to be at your fittest."

I roll my eyes in acknowledgment.

"What was that about?" Cassie asks after Nat

leaves.

"Just a private joke. At least, I hope it's a joke." She couldn't possibly hold me to the promise to strip, could she? I slip behind the counter and give Cassie's perfect backside a pat. "About time you got out of here for work, isn't it?"

"Yep." She gives me a quick peck on the mouth and heads for the door. "Dash gets his panties in a bundle when I'm late."

I walk to the door and watch her walk down the street to the Gallery.

Yes, that is definitely one perfect backside. No wonder it got assigned to follow behind the world's most perfect girl.

Epilogue

IT'S TIME TO RETURN Kevin's ashes to nature in Giles Woods before winter comes and makes the ground too hard. Cassie stayed home, but she understands why I have to be here. And she did give Robert permission to inter the ashes near the old ritual grounds. She could have refused. She owns the woods. Still, everyone understands why I'm here alone.

Natalie draws the circle for the ceremony, and I dig the hole next to the pile of stones that mark the place where Robert lay his wife's ashes so many years ago. Even though I cannot mourn Kevin, I stay within the circle when I'm done. Funerals are for the living, and my friend, Kevin's father, is still alive. I'll stay with him while he says goodbye to his son.

It's only the four of us—Robert, Natalie, Gilly, and me. Not even his buddies on the force are interested in remembering Kevin now that he's not enchanting them.

Robert places the woven cotton sack holding Kevin's ashes into the hole I'd made. It isn't deep. He pushes the loosely piled dirt over the top with his hands and wipes them on his shirt before he stands. I think this is the first time I've ever seen Robert look untidy.

When he speaks, his voice is soft, but it doesn't break.

"I know that none of you would want to speak here today about Kevin. Your memories of him aren't good. That's not your fault.

When he was young, Kevin was a quiet, studious boy. I like to remember him that way. But he was never right again after his mother died, and when Eunice took him under her wing...." Robert takes a deep breath, obviously fighting for control.

"He'll find peace in the Summerlands," Gillian says.

Robert acknowledges with a nod and continues. "I recently began to believe in gods and goddesses, although I still don't truly understand what they are. But if it's possible Kevin can pass to the Summerlands, that they, too, are something other than a metaphor...and he can be reunited with his mother before one of them moves on, then I hope he finds peace there."

"So mote it be," Gillian whispers, and Natalie echoes her.

Robert gives them a soft smile. "So mote it be."

He turns and builds a second cairn of stones over the newly disturbed earth. When he's done, Gillian gives him her hand to steady him as he rises. It's not weakness to take a hand up from a friend.

We turn away from the burial site and Gillian doesn't release his hand as they walk. Natalie glowers at them and falls a step behind.

I swear that if Natalie's brown eyes could change color to match her mood, they'd be emerald. What is going on between those three?

I shuffle along behind, not wanting to get in the middle of whatever it is they're up to. It's a good day to enjoy the peacefulness of the woods after all the danger and drama I've had here.

Cat is listening in inside my head, I know, for the rustling along the path of potential prey. I catch a sound that follows through the brush, not running away, just moving parallel to our path.

I glance to the side off and on, trying to figure out what's out there—my Cat side idling wondering how big it is and if it's any good to eat, but my Tom side wanting to know why it's shadowing us. I'm still on high alert all the time. I don't trust that any of us are safe. My life hasn't let me lower my guard much to this point.

I catch a glimpse of black against the green.

I need to know what it is.

When we reach a place where the brush thins, I bolt off through the bushes without broadcasting the move. It takes a moment before whatever's been following us to react. I'm gaining on it when a clearing opens and I see exactly what it is.

The dog turns to face me, red eyes glowing, teeth bared in a growl. Her belly is swollen, her teats engorged with milk.

I back up slowly. "Good doggy…"

The old bitch turns and lopes deeper into the woods.

ABOUT THE AUTHOR

Jill Nojack is a writer, musician and artist. The Bad Toms Series is her second published series.

When she isn't exploring her creative side, Jill enjoys laughing too loud and long in public, long bike rides, and talking about herself in third person. She resides in the great American Midwest with a long-suffering cat and makes her living as a computer tech, because, if you're lucky, that's what you do with degrees in English and Sociology.

You can visit www.jillnojack.com for more info about the series along with Jill's other books. You can also sign up for the email newsletter if you would like to be notified when new books in this and her other series are released.